YOUR PERFECT MATCH

A DOMESTIC PSYCHOLOGICAL SUSPENSE NOVEL

INA L. NARA

ISBN: 978-1-963546-13-2

WEDNESDAY, OCTOBER 21, 2099

PROLOGUE

Crowd Band Live Chat

Jimmy R: *Heard the news. Congratulations, Tony.*

My heart leaps into my throat. *What's the news?* I'm certain it doesn't involve me. I wish it did—I hope it does—but deep down, I know it doesn't.

None of them realize I'm here. I heard the chime, glanced up from the dreadful pile of papers I was grading, and there it was—a group chat I'd forgotten I was still part of.

Rebecca N: *Engaged? That was quick. Are you divorced yet?*

My heart plunges deeper into the abyss of despair.

Anthony H.: *(An extended period of dancing ellipsis.)* The divorce will be finalized soon.

Rebecca N: *(Immediate response)* Hasn't Sienna also found her match?

I, Sienna Holloway, Anthony H's wife, wait for his reply with bated breath.

Anthony H.: *(Another long stretch of dancing ellipsis.)* Yes.

I let out a shaky breath, the kind you take when the air is being knocked out of you. He lied.

Rebecca N: *Then she's happy with her new match?*

Anthony H.: *(Another long stretch of dancing ellipsis.)*

Jimmy R: *Just ask Sienna. She's in the group.*

Rebecca N: *(Dancing ellipsis)*

Before I can fully process what's happening, my phone chimes loudly, followed by a message: *You have been removed from the group.*

I clutch my stomach as the exchange and its abrupt ending send a wave of sourness rising in my throat. Beads of sweat form on my forehead, and tears blur my vision. But the real sickness lies deeper: sadness, disappointment, and heartbreak overwhelm me, forcing me to bend over and vomit into the trash can beside my desk.

SATURDAY, OCTOBER 24, 2099

CHAPTER ONE

I used to know happiness, but it feels like a distant memory now, like something that never belonged to me.

The only thing I feel is a heavy sense of dread. And not just because I arrived at this restaurant too early, leaving me with too much time to think about what I'm on the verge of doing. Honestly, I'm not in any shape to be here. I'm still a shell of my former self, thanks to Tony.

I wouldn't have initiated this process if I hadn't been for that private chat. I'm pretty sure everyone had forgotten I was part of the group between Tony and his closest friends, all of them from his "good old days" in college. The chat was initially set up to plan our extravagant New Year's Eve wedding. But even as the bride, I never chimed in. No one asked for my opinion, and I never offered it. Tony took charge of everything, making decisions for both of us. He had all the ideas, promising

7

that all I needed to do was show up as the bride of his dreams.

That's how he used to refer to me—the bride of his dreams. That was less than a year ago. Now, as I sit here, I find myself scratching my head, wondering how on earth we ended up like this.

Yes… that heart-shattering, gut-wrenching chat brought me to this seat at the bar of Urban Ember, a trendy downtown LA restaurant known for celebrity sightings and food that's pricey but not outrageously so.

Soon, I'll meet my supposed "perfect match." At least, that's what quantum matching technology claims. But as I sit on this impossibly hard bar chair, the energy coursing through me screams one undeniable truth: this match, this person I'm about to meet, cannot possibly make me feel the way Tony makes me feel.

And yet, what can I do?

Tony, *my Tony*, is with his match right now.

CHAPTER TWO

I nervously check the time on the tiny screen of my Your Perfect Match band, better known as the YPM band. This little gadget is responsible for orchestrating this entire meeting with a man named Ethan, whose last name I may finally learn when we come face to face.

Quantum Matching Inc. designed the process this way, spoon-feeding clients small doses of information about their matches as they progress through the "Meet Your Perfect Match" journey. The goal is to minimize superficial judgments and let the supposed spellbinding connection bloom naturally.

I have three minutes left to decide whether to stay or go. My heart feels like a ticking bomb. Each second feels heavier than the last as my memories drift back to the night that erased my fairytale ending.

Tony came home after meeting Tanya for the first time. I could see the shift in him immediately. His eyes were brighter, his energy high and buzzing excitedly in a way that left me feeling small and drab. Even though he swore, and still swears, that he loved me, that night, he was floating, utterly enchanted by *her*. Five days later, on August 9th, we sat at our kitchen table, and Tony asked for space.

"I need to explore this connection," he said, his voice gentle but resolute, as if inviting this *thing* into our marriage was a reasonable choice.

My throat became achingly tight as my tears threatened to spill. "Does that mean divorce?" I asked, my voice a fragile whisper.

"No, honey," Tony said, pulling me into his arms. His embrace was so familiar, so comforting, that for a moment I let myself believe nothing was wrong. Pressed against his chest, I leaned into the safety I had always found in his arms, the sense that as long as we were together, the world couldn't touch us. "I love you," he said again, his breath warm against my hair. "Why don't you meet your match? See what it feels like?" His tone was soothing, coaxing me like I was a child resisting medicine. "Maybe understanding what I'm going through will help us both."

I remember shaking my head, more tears blurring my vision. "I don't want to. I don't need to. I only want you." I was resolute, desperate. He was the one wobbling and leaving cracks in our perfect love story, not me. I believed, and *still believe*, in our happily ever after.

But maybe, after tonight, I'll feel something, anything, other than this undying love for a man and a life I can't stop clinging to. Maybe this is the beginning of the end. And maybe, just maybe, that's exactly what I need.

Or maybe not.

Maybe I should postpone this.

"Sienna?" a man's voice cuts through my decision, halting me as I slide off the stool. I freeze, torn between the urge to leave and the sudden hope tugging at me. I was ready to run, wasn't I? But now… I turn quickly toward the speaker, my eyes searching his face, desperately scanning for anything that will tell me I'll make the right choice if I stay.

"Ethan?" I swallow the lump in my throat. The name feels foreign on my lips, like a word I was never meant to speak.

"Yes, I'm Ethan," he says confidently, his smile warm and open.

Unable to stop my mind from dissecting every detail of his appearance, a flood of observations washes over me. Ethan is at least six inches shorter than Tony, his hairline showing early signs of receding. He looks older than I do by five, maybe six or seven years.

He's not unattractive, though he's no Adonis—unlike Tony, who embodies perfection. Now I understand why the service keeps photos hidden until this moment. It's not that his looks are repellant; it's just that one glance reminds me he's not Tony. No one can be my husband but my husband. For that reason alone, I know I would have dismissed him instantly.

But what am I to do now? I'm not rude. I can't simply say, *Sorry, this was a mistake on my part.* No, I can't say that. So instead, I extend my hand, keep my forced smile, and say, "Nice to meet you, Ethan."

CHAPTER THREE

E than and I settle at a table by the tall windows. Outside, the sky deepens to rich indigo as twilight dissolves into tomorrow. In the middle of the avenue, a Swift train glides by, its sleek polycarbonate body slicing effortlessly through the night as it slows for its next stop.

A few cars trail alongside the tracks, their movements leisurely compared to the train's precision and speed. Hardly anyone drives anymore—why would they when Swifts glide through every part of the city like clockwork?

Inside, the dim lighting, the soft hum of conversations, and the flickering candle between us create a cozy, almost intimate atmosphere. Yet, the weight of the moment presses down on me, keeping me from fully sinking into it.

The waiter has handed us menus, but I'm too distracted to give mine more than a cursory glance. It's packed with enticing options, and I'm genuinely starving. Then again, I'm always hungry these days. I barely eat, though. I've lost a lot of weight—at least, I think I have. I haven't stepped on a scale in years, but my clothes hang loosely now. My face looks gaunt, too. How gaunt, I wouldn't know—I can't bear to look in mirrors for more than a few seconds.

I don't want to see myself like this. Because if I fully acknowledge what I see, I'll have to accept what's happening in my life. And I don't accept it. I won't accept it.

"You should try the filet mignon encrusted with white truffle peppercorn," Ethan suggests, setting down his menu. "It's one of their most popular entrées. It's not on the menu every night, but tonight it is." His smile radiates satisfaction, as if the dish alone confirms that this evening was meant to be.

"That sounds good to me," I say, placing my menu down just as the waiter returns.

I keep my gaze on Ethan as he finalizes the order. When it comes to drinks, I choose a rosé, hoping to keep it light, while he opts for a gin and tonic.

There's a gentle way about Ethan's interactions with the waiter. He's almost caring. Tony was never overtly rude, but he carried a demanding, entitled edge that could sometimes be grating. Ethan, by contrast, is the exact opposite. And that's a plus, not a minus.

"By the way, Sienna," Ethan begins, now that the waiter has left us alone. He leans forward slightly, his expression curious, almost eager. "What's your last name?"

I shift in my seat, trying not to let my hesitation show. My mind races, weighing the decision. If I share that piece of me, does it mean we're moving forward? If I don't, does it make me seem rude?

"Holloway," I finally say, my voice steady despite the churn of thoughts inside. "And yours?"

"Ethan Clarendon. I figured we should get that out of the way, considering we've been messaging without last names. It felt a bit… impersonal." He smiles.

"Nice to meet you, Ethan Clarendon." I manage my own smile, smaller but polite.

"Are you from the city?" he asks.

"Born and raised. And you?"

"San Francisco, born and raised. LA and San Francisco aren't that far apart. That's at least one criterion met."

"Yeah," I say faintly. According to the data, matches are often supposed to have crossed paths—or at least have the potential to. But the more questions Ethan asks, the more this feels like a job interview. And the less convinced I am that he's the one.

The waiter arrives with our drinks and a large charcuterie board featuring house-baked bread, seasoned butters, and a variety of oils for dipping. We give the spread the acknowledgment it deserves, commenting, "It looks delicious. Smells incredible." Each of us takes a piece, dipping and tasting. Chew. "Mmm."

"So, what do you do for work?" Ethan asks before I can think of something to ask him.

I wish I could muster more curiosity about him. On

my first date with Tony, I couldn't stop asking questions. There was nothing I didn't want to know about him.

"I'm a lecturer," I reply, taking a generous bite of walnut bread slathered with browned butter. It's a welcome distraction; my hunger was starting to make me light-headed.

"An academic?" he presses.

I chew and nod indifferently, hoping to stall the conversation from veering toward my job.

"Where, might I ask?" he persists, unfortunately.

"UCLA. School of Law. I lecture in Environmental Justice Law," I say, grinding out the words before taking a sip of wine. I really don't want to discuss it further, but to soften the awe creeping onto his face, I add, "But I'm not a professor. They just pay me to teach classes."

"Do you like it?"

"Huh?" I blurt, caught off guard.

"Your job. Do you like it?" These days, even the thought of teaching makes my stomach churn. Last quarter's student reviews flash through my mind. Some were almost poetic: *'She has a monotone voice that lulls anyone listening to sleep.'* Others were brutally blunt: *'Passionless. Boring.'* And that was before my separation. I can't imagine what they'll say at the end of this quarter. I know I'm failing, yet I don't know how to turn it around.

"Then you don't like your job?" Ethan asks gently, nudging me back into the conversation.

I follow his gaze to my finger, tapping rhythmically on the table. I stop, feeling suddenly exposed. "I don't know. I mean…" I chuckle nervously, my voice shaky. "I really don't know."

His eyes remain steady, studying me with a quiet intensity, like I'm a portrait with hidden depths. The longer he looks, the more I feel like he's seeing past my words, reading between lines I didn't even realize I'd drawn. It's unnerving. I shift in my seat, uncomfortable, yet also curious. What is he picking up on that I think I'm hiding so well?

The longer he holds that gaze, the more my impatience grows. "What is it?" I snap, sharper than I intended.

His lips curl into a slow smile. "So…"

"So, what?" I ask, shaking my head, confused.

"Is this a crock of shit or what?"

It takes a moment for his words to land, but when they do, the tension shatters. He's just masterfully broken the ice, and laughter bursts from me—sudden, hearty, and real. I haven't laughed like this in ages. A weight lifts, the pressure easing for the first time in what feels like forever. It's liberating, but also a little disappointing.

"I really wanted to have faith in the process, but…" I shrug, letting the truth settle between us.

"It's odd, though," Ethan says, his frown deepening. "Everyone I know who used YPM found *the one*. I really thought…" He trails off, pressing his lips together, the weight of disappointment evident.

His letdown is almost palpable, and I feel a pang of sympathy. He came here genuinely believing in this process, in finding his perfect match, and now that hope is slipping away. I've always been skeptical of YPM's impressive success rate, even though, as a lawyer, I've combed through the fine print. No lawsuits, no false advertising claims—just solid numbers. Still, I'm surprised too. Ethan and I aren't a match. But unlike him, I already know love.

My thoughts drift back to Tony and our New Year's Eve wedding; his smile could light up my world, which makes him special in my eyes. He's everything I still crave.

"I don't know," I whisper, my voice thick with longing. "I just miss my husband."

Ethan blinks, as if struck by a sudden gust of wind. "You're married?" His eyes widen, shock and confusion etched across his face.

"Sorry. If we were still together, I wouldn't be here. Our divorce is final at the end of the month, whether I want it or not." The disappointment in my voice is unmistakable, and I cringe internally. I'm supposed to be pretending everything is fine. I'm fine. This is all fucking fine.

"I see," Ethan replies, rubbing the stubble on his cheek. The easy smile he's worn all night fades, replaced by something more serious.

Guilt tightens my chest. I feel like I've lured him into something false, something misleading. "Do you still want to have dinner?" I ask, my voice uncertain. "I'd understand if you don't."

He hesitates, then lets out a soft sigh. "No… I mean, yes," he finally says, a touch of disappointment lingering in his tone. "It's nice to be out tonight, but if you're ready to call it quits, I won't be offended. I'll stay and eat my steak, though, and I'll have yours boxed up to go. You have to try it, Sienna. This meal is legendary."

And just like that—my smile, my snorting chuckle—they're both real. It's been forever since I felt this light, like stepping out of a suffocating fog and into the sun.

"No," I say, shaking my head, then quickly correct myself. "I mean, yes. I'll stay."

CHAPTER FOUR

E than's eyes taper thoughtfully. "Can I ask you something?"

Even though the pressure feels lighter now, I still brace myself, raising my wine glass to my lips. "Sure." I take a drink

"Did you and your husband see someone before activating your YPM bands?"

The question catches me off guard. I slowly lower my glass, my brow furrowing. "What do you mean by 'see someone'?"

"A therapist," he clarifies, leaning in, his eyes locked on mine, unwavering.

I freeze. "A therapist?"

"A licensed marriage and family therapist, to be exact."

His words land between us, heavy and unexpected.

"Oh," I say, as an image of Tony and me sitting stiffly across from a therapist flashes through my mind. The therapist is faceless, sexless—a neutral figure trying to save us. "I never thought about that," I admit quietly. "Maybe we should have."

"You should have," he insists. "It's required."

His words hit me like a punch to the gut. *Required?* My mind scrambles, replaying our final days. Everything happened so fast—too fast. Tony and I made so many rushed decisions, each one pulling us further apart.

A therapist could've forced us to slow down. Maybe I could've convinced him to never bring those YPM bands home in the first place. Instead, we wore them and spiraled, each in our own direction. The distance grew into an abyss, swallowing the beautiful love story that once defined us, the very reason he got down on one knee.

Is it too late to make him see a therapist with me? The idea flares in my mind, sudden and desperate. I'm sure I can convince him. He loves me more than he loves her. I know this because, just a day before I saw that awful group chat, he told me, *"Don't worry about us yet, Sienna. I still love you."*

I'm still baffled, lost in the sanctuary of my own thoughts, as our entrées are placed before us. The server lingers at the edge of the table, announcing that, alongside the filet mignon, we have sautéed mushrooms over roasted corn and potato hash. But not even the heavenly aroma wafting from the dish can quiet the storm raging within me. I can't stop thinking about the possibilities. I can't stall the question looping endlessly through my mind.

What can I do...
What can I do...

What can I do?

The waiter's cheery "Enjoy!" barely registers as he waltzes off, leaving Ethan and me alone in the dim glow of candlelight.

"You okay?" Ethan's voice cuts through my swirling thoughts.

The truth? "I don't know," I confess. Ethan's eyebrows furrow slightly, and I add, almost as an afterthought, "I don't think there's a universe where Tony would ever"—I draw air quotes—"'lower himself' to see a therapist. In his mind, there's nothing wrong with him or any decision he makes."

Anger flashes through me, brief but hot. It isn't a new feeling, but this time, it lingers longer than usual. I imagine yelling at Tony, though the words are unclear, incoherent. I don't even know what I'd say.

"And in your book?" Ethan asks, casually slicing into his steak, the blade gliding through like butter.

His nonchalance rubs me the wrong way. "What do you mean?"

"In your book, is there nothing wrong with him?" He chews calmly, as if his question isn't profound. But it is. It makes me circle my shoulders to loosen them, like I'm pushing against an invisible weight.

"What? Are you a therapist?" I snap, the words sharper than I intended. Bitterness rises, leaving a defensive taste in my mouth.

Ethan presses his lips together, his expression unreadable. "Actually, I am."

My jaw drops. "You're kidding."

"Nope," he says, taking another bite.

Could this night get any stranger? The absurdity of it all overwhelms me, and laughter bursts out of me, sudden, uncontrollable, rising to a fever pitch. I don't know whether to blame fate, karma, or some cosmic force for screwing with me. Is this supposed to break me? Push me to get help? Or maybe just force me to let go?

Or maybe it wants me to really see the mess my life has become. Tony meets his match, falls head over heels, and is now planning a wedding. I meet my match, feel nothing, and it turns out he's a shrink? And to top it off, I learn this entire nightmare could've been avoided if Tony and I had followed the rules and seen someone like Ethan before the bands were ever activated. If we had, I wouldn't be here.

Finally, on a deep exhale, I manage to stop laughing, wiping the tears from my eyes.

Ethan tilts his head, watching me curiously. "Glad you found it amusing. I would've disclosed my profession earlier, but we were busy chasing other topics."

"It's fine," I say, waving a hand with exaggerated indifference. But the urge to explain myself bubbles up. "Knowing Tony, I doubt he even knew about the therapist requirement," I add quickly. "We didn't get our bands the usual way. Tony's a lead software integration engineer for White Glove Team Technology, and Quantum Matching Inc. contracted him to develop some of the YPM band's features."

Ethan grunts thoughtfully, his gaze shifting into something more analytical, which makes me feel like I need to keep explaining.

I stab at my food, eating quickly, as if the words need to come out before I lose my appetite. "Anyway, he introduced the bands, and I agreed too easily. I honestly never thought they'd work. I never believed all that 'perfect match' nonsense. I barely even noticed quantum matching technology existed until it tore my life apart. I should've said no."

Ethan's eyes remain steady, studying me like he's trying to read between the lines. "So, you're saying it's all your fault?"

I straighten, jarred by the unexpected question. "What?"

"The collapse of your marriage," he clarifies. "Do you feel it's your fault?"

"Umm…" I say, my gaze shifting out the window to a group of people walking by, their faces forward, one of them animatedly leading the conversation. My mind drifts, overlaying the scene with a memory I've tried to forget—a dinner a few months before the separation.

Tony had surprised me with two small white boxes that looked like they were from a high-end jeweler. The elegantly designed "YPM" logo on each box caught my eye. *Ooh*, I'd gasped, dazzled by what I thought would be a beautiful gold necklace or some other piece of fine jewelry. I still remember his long, graceful fingers carefully peeling open the lids, his movements deliberate, as if he were about to present me with the rarest of diamonds. But they weren't diamonds. They were bands.

Why am I hesitating? Of course, it's my fault. It has to be. I'm the one who has to fix this mess.

"I think so," I finally manage to say. Then, more firmly, "Yes. He gave me an option, and I said yes. I shouldn't have given my consent."

Ethan's clinical gaze remains locked on my face, assessing. The scrutiny makes me want to shrink, but then something inside me hardens. I straighten my posture because I meant my answer. Yes, it's my fault. I could've shown Tony how much I wanted only him by insisting we throw those bands in the trash. He was just doing his job, excited about testing a client's product.

"Sienna," Ethan says too tenderly, too sympathetically, "how about you visit me at my office? We can talk this through in a more appropriate setting." He nods toward the bustling restaurant, a clear gesture that this trendy place, with its delicious food, is no place for therapy.

His offer makes me bristle with rage, but I force a polite smile. Ethan is a nice guy, and I'm a nice girl. I'd like to keep things that way. When I decline his offer, I won't let him see how I really feel. But beneath the surface, there's something else, something desperate, something hidden, something I should be ashamed of.

CHAPTER FIVE

Yes, I had politely declined Ethan's offer, but he still withdrew a silver-cased cardholder from the top pocket of his crisp light blue shirt and handed me his business card. "Call if you ever feel the need to talk. And don't worry about my rate. I'll waive my three hundred an hour for you. It's the least I can do after this service got it so wrong."

Still, the mention of his hourly fee made me pause. That's a lot of money, I thought, realizing Ethan must be exceptionally skilled at what he does. Too bad I don't need his services. What I need is my old life back.

Ethan shook his head, clearly baffled. He seemed genuinely surprised that our match had fizzled. With YPM boasting a near-perfect success rate, we were apparently part of that tiny percentage whose energies resulted in a "dull" match.

"However, our bands can be recalibrated, and we could wear them for another six weeks…" he began.

I cut him off, raising my hand. "It's okay, Ethan. You don't owe me anything."

Although part of me thought, *Six weeks? Tony said we needed to wear them for two months.*

Ethan didn't retreat. He held his card out, insistent. "Sienna, take it. Please. It's the least I can do. Plus, it would be negligent of me not to offer my assistance through your grieving process. Let me help you."

Hearing him say I'm in a "grieving process" threw me for another loop. He'd thrown me for so many over the course of the night that I felt like I was tied in knots.

Sure, I know there are supposed to be seven stages of grief before you come to terms with a loss, but that doesn't apply to me.

I will get what I want.

There's no way Tony won't come back to me.

If tonight proved anything, it's that quantum matching is complete bullshit.

But to appease Ethan, I took the card and offered a quick, "Sure, I'll call if necessary," knowing full well I never would.

Before we left, Ethan assured me he'd raise a support ticket for a full analysis of our match.

"Wouldn't hurt," he said, watching for my agreement.

I forced a tight smile, masking my indifference as best I could. "I guess not."

We exchanged email addresses, just in case his support ticket yielded any updates worth sharing. After that, we said our goodbyes, and I watched him walk away.

And now, here I am, hidden among the thick green foliage, branches poking into every inch of my body. I ask myself the same question every time I do this: *Should I really be standing in the tall privacy hedges lining Tony's eleven-million-dollar home in The Bird Streets?*

It's a ridiculous amount for a house, but Tony can afford it. With his executive salary, end-of-year bonuses, and contract work, he brings in an average of six million a year. It took him five years of saving nearly every penny to buy this place. He haggled the builder down from thirteen million and somehow managed to get it for eleven. He wasn't even the highest bidder, but Tony always wins. He never shares how he does it—he just does it.

"I always get what I want," he used to say, and it's precisely why I need him so much. With Tony, I always felt secure, like I'd never have to long for anything I couldn't have.

Yes, it's his confidence, his magnetic presence. I used to watch him in awe. Waking up beside him, making love to him, even something as simple as observing him brush his teeth or slipping into one of his perfectly tailored suits, it all felt like I was watching a performance. And I was his only spectator, his biggest admirer.

But here I am, defying every shred of dignity I have left to stand here like this, hidden among the thick foliage. The journey here was a precise operation, a set of logistics I've come to rely on. I took the Swift home, then drove straight to this spot.

Exhausted? Yes. But tonight's events pushed me over the edge.

I had to come.

CHAPTER SIX

I t's 9:49 p.m. The sprinklers will start in eleven minutes. I've let them drench me before, once, on a night when Tony and Tanya were entertaining guests. Six couples, including themselves. They must've been her friends because I didn't recognize any of them. I thought I knew all of Tony's friends, or at least, I used to.

I couldn't look away as Tony and Tanya laughed and touched each other like they were one body, perfectly in sync, basking in their own performance. Tanya rested her head on his shoulder, her hand brushing his chest, while Tony ran his fingers through her hair. Then they kissed. Their guests seemed spell-bound, mesmerized by the facade of ideal coupledom.

But as I watched, I caught glimpses of holes in their act. Tony's gaze drifted at times. When nobody was looking, Tanya would nudge him after he spoke, a subtle chastisement in her expression. He'd return the look, tight-lipped. No, they weren't the perfect couple they pretended to be. If nobody else could see it, I could.

Tanya doesn't live with Tony, or so he says. When I asked if she'd moved in, he was quick to tell me no. But she's been at his house constantly since the Thursday before last, moving around like she owns the place. And she doesn't behave like a guest, either. Guests spend time with their hosts, sharing the same spaces. Not her.

She often exists in her own world, tucked away in the upstairs den for hours, probably watching TV or scrolling on her phone. Once, I saw her standing in the window, phone in hand, gaze fixed on the yard. Her eyes seemed locked on the very spot where I stood, and for a moment, I thought she could sense me. But she didn't see me.

Tony spends most of his time in his office, though less so now that Tanya's around. They have a lot of sex. They're like magnets, tangled up on the front porch, on the lawn, as if the privacy hedges could shield them.

I've watched him go down on her in the stairwell, pressed against the wall, and he's none the wiser to the blank look that sometimes crosses her face. Maybe she's a good actress, or maybe he's just too wrapped up to notice.

When they're not together, he retreats to his office. I can't see it from here, but I know it well. From experience, I know it's his escape.

Tonight, the upstairs den, her space, is dark, but lights glow softly in the living room. A warm haze spills from the kitchen and filters through the house, lighting the floating staircase that curves gracefully up to the second floor. It's clear he's not home.

The question nags at me: *Where is he? Are they together? Has he read the text I sent him?* These thoughts gnaw at me, endless and relentless. I'd written it and hit send while riding the Swift, but unless he replies, I won't know if he's seen it. Tony's always kept his phone settings private —no read receipts. I hated that quirk of his then, and I hate it even more now.

I swipe at a tickling sensation on my neck. Insects buzz all around me; I get bitten every time I do this, but I don't care.

I could go inside if I wanted to. I could walk through my old home as though nothing had changed. Tony hasn't updated the security codes, and my fingerprint still unlocks every door. I know because I checked the security website—I still have access. Maybe he's so caught up in juggling this new life that he forgot to tie up the loose ends of his old one. Or maybe… maybe he still loves me. Maybe he still needs to hold onto some part of me while he "sorts out" this quantum match mess.

Quantum matching feels like a dark spell cast over everything, sinister and binding. Every part of me wishes I'd never agreed to try it.

Just as I brace myself to leave the cover of the hedges, my phone vibrates in my coat pocket. My heart lurches, pounding against my ribs like it wants out.

I have a new text message.

It's him.

It *has* to be him.

CHAPTER SEVEN

TONY

We're at The Peabody on Sunset Boulevard, an impressive restaurant with a reputation to match. Dinner was served under that warm, dull orange lighting that hangs over everything like a haze. The booths, upholstered in red leather and curved into semicircles, offer just enough privacy for a table of four. The food was better than expected—decent, even—but now, as we linger over after-dinner drinks, the conversation is wearing thin.

I'm itching to leave. Honestly, it's Sara's laugh that's doing me in. The sound grinds into my ears like a drill —half donkey's bray, half barn owl's screech. Every time she cackles, it takes everything in me not to wince.

I glance down at my phone, hoping for a message, anything to pull me away. But Tanya nudges my arm, urging me back into the conversation. She doesn't care about Sara's latest rambling story; I know she just wants me to focus on *him*.

Alexander Creston. *The* Alexander Creston. I can

hardly believe I'm sitting at the same table with him in this capacity—a man whose name is synonymous with unimaginable wealth. Yes, wealth passed down, not earned. But if you listen to Sara, Alexander is some kind of brilliant, self-made entrepreneur who "started from the ground up."

Not so. Not fucking so.

"We hit a rough patch on the vessel crossing the…" Sara pauses, laughing again as her eyes dart toward Alexander like he's the eighth wonder of the world. "Where were we, Alexander?" She snaps her fingers, fishing for his answer.

"The Western Mediterranean," he replies smoothly, his expression indifferent.

Too cool for school, that's the vibe Alexander gives off. The fake charm, the aloof half-smile. It's all an act. Everyone at this table is falling for it.

But not me.

"Isn't your vessel more of a superyacht?" I ask, keeping my tone light, though I feel the corners of my mouth twitch in a barely restrained sneer. I don't want to sound hostile, but his pretension grates on me. *Vessel*, as if he's some intrepid explorer charting the seas with purpose, not just cruising around, living it up without a care in the world.

Tanya shoots me a subtle look, a warning not to push too far. But I hold my ground, emboldened by the flicker of irritation stirring inside me.

"No, no," Sara insists, shaking her head with the fervor of a true disciple. "Alexander is a philanthropist, Tony."

"Anthony," I correct, my voice nearly a growl. If she insists on calling him Alexander, then she can get my name right, too.

Sara's head jerks up, stunned. Her reaction's valid—we're equals, colleagues in the same division, just on different teams. I usually keep things civil, wouldn't even bother correcting her. Usually, I even like her.

But something about this scene—her nonstop praise of him, his haughty indifference, Tanya's watchful gaze —sets my insides on fire.

No, I'm not bitter. I'm not jealous, no matter what Tanya keeps implying with her little remarks and innu-endos. It's not jealousy. There's just something about *this guy* that gets to me.

"He's not good enough, that's all," I'd once told Tanya.

"For who? Sara?" she'd shot back with a laugh. "Honey, she hit the YPM mega jackpot, okay?"

"Uh-huh," I'd muttered, brushing it off. But Tanya just kept laughing, tossing her head like I was the punch-line to some private joke.

If I hadn't been so distracted by the curve of her neck and the urge to touch her, I might've walked out of the bedroom. Instead, I stayed, giving her every reason to remember she'd hit her own jackpot with me.

I bring charm, ambition, and actual personality. This guy? He's as exciting as a tax return. Any woman would see it in under an hour. If Sara would stop talking long enough to notice how little he actually says, she'd get bored with him too.

"Okay," I say, resting my arm on the table and

leaning in, locking eyes with him. Time to cut through the haze. "Isn't your father Christian Creston?"

"Yes," he replies, his eyes narrowing slightly, as if trying to gauge where I'm going. But he knows. We all do.

A smug smile creeps onto my face, and I don't bother hiding it. "I'm thinking he's the reason—"

"Hold on," Sara interrupts, jumping in on cue, right on schedule. "Alexander has a doctorate in International Relations and Diplomacy. He speaks seven languages, Tony. He collaborates with governments to build hurricane-resistant communities, not to mention the vessel. It's designed to carry almost as much as a small cargo ship and is practically unsinkable. Assuming he's just living off his father's money is, well... rude."

Alex raises a hand, and Sara instantly falls silent, like a trained pet waiting for her next cue. It's almost amusing. He could stop this parade of praise any time he wanted, but he doesn't. He chooses not to.

He turns back to me, his gaze sharpening. "It's fine," he says, his voice lowering as he locks in on me. "Call me Alex. It doesn't matter. It's just a name."

Sara grunts in disapproval, rolling her eyes like she's offended on his behalf. It's clear she's irritated by his casual offer.

"I agree—it's just a name, *Alex*," I reply, letting the name linger in a way I know will grate on her. It's petty, but I savor the small satisfaction.

Tanya nudges my ankle under the table—a silent reminder to ease up—but I'm past caring. Pleasantries are off the table.

Alex nods slightly, as if acknowledging some simple truth. "Also, you're not entirely wrong. Financially, I had a leg up."

"But," Tanya chimes in, her voice honeyed, "you could've just as easily done nothing, right? Lived comfortably off your father's wealth, and yet... here you are." Of course, she's right there with the flattery, practically putting a second set of lip prints on his ass.

"In my family, doing nothing was never an option," Alex replies coolly. "But yes, I was able to choose my own path."

"And he's met so many people along that path," Sara interjects, launching into yet another monologue, this time name-dropping actors and actresses she's met "through his work." Does she even hear herself?

Tanya laughs, a little too loudly, feigning delight at the mention of Brittany Loeb. Then she leans closer to me, her breath warm against my ear. "Knock it off," she whispers.

I force a friendly expression, giving Alex my best smile. "So, is that what you're doing in LA? Hobnobbing?"

"Actually," Sara cuts in—again—rubbing her palms together like she's delivering the climax of some grand reveal. "Alexander's setting off next year, traveling the world, saving vulnerable communities. Since he won't be sailing the Pacific for an entire year, he's hosting a huge New Year's Eve bash, sailing from San Pedro Harbor up the coast to San Francisco. The route is in honor of our 'magnificent body of water.' And, of course, you're both invited."

"We have—" I start, ready to decline.

But Tanya's hand tightens on my shoulder. "Thank you, both. We'd love to come," she says, her voice loud enough to drown out any protest I might've made. Then, turning to Sara, she adds with a knowing smile, "But what about you two? You're matched—are you really going to do long distance? I can't imagine doing long distance with mine."

She leans into me, her touch meant to soothe, and, to my surprise, it works. My irritation cools, if only a little.

Alex is watching me now, intently, his gaze sharp and searching, like he's trying to figure something out.

Sara, oblivious to the exchange, takes another sip of her martini and settles back into the red leather seat. "I've got a lot lined up," she says. "My team landed Fresco Group, and we start their project first thing in January."

But Alex's gaze doesn't shift. It stays on me, steady and unyielding. He probably thinks he can see right through me, read me down to my core.

Well, he can't, and he never will.

Damn, I hate that guy.

CHAPTER EIGHT

TONY

The car ride home was mostly silent. Tanya stayed glued to her phone, giving me the cold shoulder because she thinks I embarrassed her. Now, upstairs in the bedroom, I peel off my Leonhart cotton-silk shirt carefully, trying not to snag the material, though deep down, I want to rip it off.

Meanwhile, Tanya, already out of her dress and sliding her stockings down her legs, is waiting for me to explain why I treated "poor Alexander" so unfairly.

"You can call him Alex," I remind her, an edge creeping into my voice.

She scoffs, folding her stockings neatly before tucking them into one of the drawers I set aside for her. "He's never told anyone to call him Alex or Alexander. That's all Sara's doing."

"He could've stopped her."

"But he's too classy, too considerate to do that."

I let out a sharp, mocking laugh.

She slaps my arm lightly, then flops onto the edge of the bed. "You're an asshole, Tony."

I glance over. She's sitting there with her arms folded tightly across her chest, clearly mad. She's closed off, her body language tense. And here I am, wanting her to open up. In her black lace lingerie against her creamy brown skin, she's irresistible, tempting me beyond measure.

I rub my chin, choosing my words carefully. This might sting, but still, I say, "Sorry, baby. That wasn't fair."

"Then explain your issue with Alexander…or should I say Alex?" Her eyes glint with playful challenge as she leans back, grinning, every bit seductive. "Other than the fact he's rich, has rich and famous friends, and a big, big boat? Oh, and let's be honest, looks-wise, you're about neck and neck."

I hold her gaze, fighting the urge to turn my stare into daggers. But she's too enticing, and I crave her more than I'd like to admit. I can't help but wonder: *Is that the core of our so-called 'quantum match'? Just unbridled, overpowering lust?*

Tanya scoots up, pressing her back against the headboard, folding her legs beneath her. "By the way, who were you texting during dinner? Sienna?" Her tone is casual, but her eyes betray her curiosity.

"It was James," I say, slipping out of my pants and draping them neatly over the bench at the foot of the bed. I should probably hang them in the closet, but right now, I don't want to waste a second more. I climb onto the bed, moving toward her. Tanya's gaze grows hazy with need as she separates her knees, her body language unmistakably inviting.

"And what did James want on a Saturday night?" she asks, her voice soft, even as the air thickens between us, laced with desire.

"Something about programming," I murmur, brushing my lips to hers, pulling her into a long, deep kiss. Her body responds, her energy syncing with mine in a way that's almost tangible. The weight of the evening lifts as our bodies align, her pulse matching mine.

I can feel her unspoken questions, her lingering doubts, but I know exactly what she needs to hear. "You don't ever have to worry about my soon-to-be ex-wife, sexy," I whisper, my voice thick with conviction. "I'm all yours."

It's all she needs. Her doubts dissolve in an instant, and she opens up completely, surrendering to me as I take her fully.

MONDAY, OCTOBER 26, 2099

CHAPTER NINE

I stop tapping my foot against the floor, forcing myself to be still. My nerves are stretched so thin they feel ready to snap, but I shove the thought aside.

Saturday night flashes back in vivid detail. Just as I was about to slip away from the hedges surrounding Tony's house, my phone buzzed.

He'd finally replied to my text.

> Tony My Love: Saturday, 9:51 PM
>
> Meet me at Neon Spice on Monday at 1:30 p.m.

The words were so simple, but they lit me up through and through. I clung to them like a lifeline, replaying them over and over. *"Meet me at Neon Spice on Monday at 1:30 p.m."*

And now, here I am, sitting at a table in the trendy café on Westwood Boulevard. I arrived fifteen minutes early—I couldn't help it. I've been craving this moment all weekend, the impatience gnawing at me, making it hard to sleep and impossible to eat.

But the restlessness won't ease—not until I see his gorgeous face. Not until I breathe in that bewitching scent of his, the one that lingers in my mind like a dream.

Before leaving for work this morning, I forced myself to stand in front of the mirror—to really see myself and try to make myself look better. It wasn't easy, but I was determined. As much as I hate to admit it, I am competing with her.

It was painful, studying my reflection. I couldn't look away, even though I wanted to. Puffy, tired eyes. Dull, lifeless skin. The heaviness in my lids. This face has become my norm since Tony and I separated, and I don't know how to fix it, except by doing what I'm doing now: trying to get my life back.

Still, I knew I could make a better case for us if I tried to pretty myself up. So, I brushed on some powder, added a few eyedrops, swiped on lipstick, and combed my hair into a neat bun. When I finally stepped out of my apartment, I felt… passable.

But my nerves are frayed, and tension drags up endless memories. Saturday night dinner with Ethan didn't spark anything romantic, but it planted another seed of hope. Since then, I've been replaying my practiced lines over and over—the words I'll say to make Tony see the light:

"Tony, we've been married less than a year. We made a life commitment to each other. We owe it to ourselves to see a therapist before finalizing our divorce."

I wanted to add, *"Don't you think?"* But I know better than to end with a question. For better results, favorable ones, I need to keep my statement simple and clear. Encourage action. Don't inspire him to question the action I'm encouraging.

It's going to work, I tell myself as my eyes flick back to my phone, watching the seconds tick by.

Three minutes until our scheduled lunch, and the waitress asks if I'm ready to order. I tell her my husband will be here soon, and we'll order together—m*y husband.* I loved saying that.

But Tony does better than "soon." He arrives less than two minutes before our scheduled time. I spot him the moment his tall, commanding frame steps through the doorway. A surge of joy hits me, a wave of happiness so intense it's almost overwhelming. I raise my hand to wave, but he's already scanning the room, his brows knitted with that familiar intensity, forming a deep crease between his eyes. So serious. So effortlessly handsome.

He spots me. I sit up straighter, drawn to him as he strides through the restaurant with that casual confidence, turning heads in his wake.

I take in his outfit, because I always love what he wears. Today, it's a black cashmere duster coat—all his coats are either cashmere or leather—paired with perfectly tailored charcoal gray pants. He's incomparable, like a figure out of myth, untouchable in his beauty and presence.

And yet, he's my Tony. My husband. The man who,

without quantum energy or technology, fell in love with me, genuinely, naturally. *Not her.*

Without thinking, I rise effortlessly as he reaches our table. His arm curls around me, pulling me close, and he kisses my cheek. His lips are a familiar warmth, one that eases the restlessness inside me, if only for a few precious heartbeats.

CHAPTER TEN

"You're early," he says, his mouth pressing down at the corners, a flicker of frustration crossing his face as he takes his seat.

He's always loathed my habit of being early. In his mind, showing up early is a guaranteed way to fade into the scenery—forgettable, ordinary, unworthy of attention. He's told me that more times than I can count, and his words usually sting. But today, the ache doesn't come. I'm too thrilled to see him to let his polished disapproval touch me.

I smile, meeting his gaze. "So are you," I tease.

He leans forward slightly, giving me a playful glare, a silent acknowledgment that my response has earned me a small, insignificant win. Touché.

Tony's lips part, as if he's about to speak, but his gaze lingers, drifting slowly over my face. I resist the urge to fidget, settling instead for a quick swipe at my cheek, hoping my face powder is blended well enough to hide the dark circles under my eyes. "I haven't been sleeping well," I say, breaking the silence, though I know what I see in his eyes isn't concern—it's judgment. I don't look like the woman he married. That much is true. But how can he not know? He's the reason I've become this.

He grunts in response, a barely-there sound, and lifts a finger to signal the waitress. I watch, an eager spectator to the performance of his effortless gestures. He shrugs off his coat, revealing the soft gleam of its black silk lining. His cologne, Radar by Jon Gar, glides through the air between us, stirring up memories: the same scent on the pillow next to mine, the warmth of his skin so close it once made my head spin.

The waitress arrives, her bright smile fixed firmly on Tony. It doesn't waver. She's barely older than the students in my first-year seminars. When I was her age, I'd never have flirted with a man Tony's age—well, unless he was Tony.

"I'll have the Korean barbecue tacos," Tony says smoothly, like he's ordering on autopilot. Then his gaze flicks to me. "She'll have… the curry-spiced lamb burger?"

My voice, softened by the weight of emotion, answers, "Yes." A part of me melts at how he still remembers my usual. *This is love,* I think, watching him. *Isn't it?* Someone who still knows these small things, who holds onto the details that matter. If that's not love, I don't know what is.

"For sides, we'll have the truffle-sesame fries and spicy pickled veggies," he adds.

I love those fries.

The waitress thanks us and turns off the hologram menu hovering over the center of our table. Neither of us needed it; our order is already a worn-in habit, like so many things between us.

"So…" He leans back, one eye narrowing as he studies me. "What's this I hear about seeing a therapist?"

My eyebrows lift instinctively. Of course Tony would get straight to the point, his tone tinged with that familiar edge of impatience. Dismissive, almost mocking. It's clear he doesn't plan on taking the requirement seriously.

As a lawyer, I've never argued a single case before a judge or jury. While earning my degree, I taught countless undergraduate law classes for the department, and I was good enough at it to never stop. But now, in this moment, I'm on the verge of arguing my first case—a case that could make or break me.

I adjust in my chair, my posture straightening. "We were required to undergo therapy before even wearing YPM bands. That didn't happen." I let the words hang in the air, an open-ended invitation for other possibilities to follow—like, *and we should,* or the subtle suggestion that this requirement could serve as legal grounds to pause the divorce and insist we fulfill it.

Tony thrusts his chin up, his words sharp and pointed as he demands, "Who told you this?"

"I texted you to let you know I was meeting my match on Saturday, and the fact that I'm still married came up." I tilt my head slightly, a hint of curiosity softening my expression. "I assumed then—and I still do now—that you didn't know anything about this stip-ulation?"

I purposely phrase my words as a declarative ques-tion. It could be taken as either a statement or an inquiry, depending on how Tony chooses to interpret it.

But the tension in his posture, the way his shoulders set back like he's ready for a fight, makes me question that assumption. The energy radiating from him isn't neutral—it's undeniably hostile.

"I remember your text. And no, I didn't know," he says, the flash of hostility in his tone deflating like a balloon losing air. He rubs his chin, his expression pensive. Watching him, it hits me like an epiphany: I rely on reading all of Tony's subtle gestures far more than I realized. But why? I can't fully explain—maybe the answer lies somewhere in what's happening between us right now.

"The divorce…" I begin, pushing forward even though every instinct screams to let it go, to enjoy the fragile peace of one of our favorite restaurants.

"I've been thinking about that," he says.

Relief washes over me, and I know, truly know, he's about to say something I desperately want to hear.

"I miss you, Sienna." His gaze softens, and his eyes are filled with a familiar tenderness. "Seeing you here today reminds me how much I still love you."

I can't stop nodding, my heart so full it feels like it might overflow. I believe him. I truly do. But one ques-tion presses against my mind, a question that's haunted me for weeks, turning even my dreams into nightmares.

"I saw the messages from the chat group—the one

we set up for our wedding," I begin cautiously. Other questions flood my mind, crashing in too fast to contain: *Why was I so swiftly deleted from the group once you realized I was still in it? Were you trying to hide something from me?* But I push them aside and ask the one that matters most. "Are you really asking her to marry you?"

The words leave me breathless. It feels like I'm outside myself, hovering above our table, a silent observer, waiting for his answer to either shatter or save me.

"No," he says, his voice steady, filled with conviction. I can't bring myself to doubt him. "Especially not now. Because, as I said, sitting here with you reminds me how much I love you, Sienna."

His gaze shifts, unfocused, as he shakes his head, the weight of everything visibly pressing down on him. It's as if he's carrying the same turmoil I've been feeling, mirroring my own inner chaos. My heart swells, clinging to a fragile glimmer of hope.

"Why don't we try therapy first?" I suggest, sensing he might be open, willing to do what it takes to bring us back to where we were.

Tony's eyes meet mine, steady and intense. "No therapy, baby. But how about we put any talk of divorce on hold until the end of the year? Let's see if this"—he places a hand over his heart, his gesture as if to quiet something restless within—"fades away."

Words form and scatter in my mind like broken puzzle pieces, but I stay silent, processing.

Then, almost as if he's convincing himself, he adds, "I think it's already starting to."

I edge closer, my focus solely on him, the world narrowing to this one moment. "Is it?"

His fingers tap softly against the table, and for the first time, I see a sliver of vulnerability in him—a quiet hesitation I've never witnessed before.

Our food arrives, but the fragrant dishes barely register. All I feel is the stirring of hope, filling spaces I'd thought were long empty. Could Tony and I find our way back to what we once had—sooner rather than later?

"Enjoy," the waitress says, her dazzled eyes lingering a little too long on my husband.

"Thank you," Tony replies, his effortless charm weaving its spell again. It's second nature to him—an art he's perfected without trying.

As soon as she's out of sight, I lean forward, my hands gripping the edge of the table as if it might steady me. The words tumble out before I can stop them, shaky and raw. "What if I just move back home? You're already paying half my rent anyway. I could... I could sleep in a guest room. Just until... until you figure out whatever it is you need."

My voice cracks on the last word, and it hangs heavy in the air, pleading. *Please hear me. Please let this work.*

"Sienna, no."

The firmness in his voice jolts me, and I go still. My appetite vanishes as tears blur my vision. It's as though a wound I thought I'd grown numb to has split open, flooding me with raw heartbreak.

"Sienna..." he sighs, breaking the silence. Slowly,

Tony reaches across the table, his hand grazing mine before wrapping it in a gentle, insistent hold.

I'm transfixed, barely breathing, as he stands and guides me to my feet. Right here, in a room full of lunch diners, Tony folds me into a steady, soothing embrace. It's like he's anchoring me, holding me in place when I feel like falling apart.

"I'm confused," he whispers near my ear, his breath warm and steady. "And marrying Tanya? That's not even an option right now, because I'm still married to you."

He pauses, his arms tightening around me. "I'm sorry for all the havoc I've caused you. I truly am. But I'm here, Sienna. I'm not going anywhere."

Then he leans in, pressing a tender kiss to my lips, lingering just long enough to let the message sink in. When he pulls back, his gaze meets mine, piercing, full of something I thought I'd lost.

In his eyes, I see everything: his love, his apology, his silent plea for patience. It's all there.

If I can hold on a little longer, he'll come back to me. And I will. I'll wait for him, for as long as it takes.

CHAPTER ELEVEN

On the MWT, a long stretch of moving walkway tracks suspended above the ground sidewalks, I'm riding high. The afternoon chill barely fazes me; I'm too wrapped up in the warmth of hope. The path ahead leads back to the university, with convenient stops along the way, but all I can think about is Tony. His kiss lingers on my lips, and the optimism coursing through me is enough to ignore the cold air slipping through my wool coat and down the neckline of my blouse.

My phone vibrates in my hand, and I step onto the standing-only belt of the MWT, my heart leaping. *It's Tony.* It has to be. Maybe he's texting to say he loves me or reassuring me to hold onto my faith in us.

But as I glance at the screen, my stomach plummets. It's not Tony.

It's a notification from Ethan, messaging me through the YPM app.

I hover over the *Do Not Accept* button, my thumb poised. A part of me wants to sever the last thread of YPM connectivity between us, to close the chapter entirely. I would much rather Ethan email me—anything to avoid that app.

But then, I'm riding this wave of possibility, feeling like life is finally tipping in my favor. And Ethan? Even though there was no spark, he's a good guy. I genuinely like him.

With a flick of my thumb, I tap: *Accept.*

> Ethan Clarendon: 3:05 PM
>
> Thank you for staying and having dinner with me on Saturday night. It was a pleasure meeting you, Sienna. I still believe there may have been an error in our dull match—these things happen occasionally. I've already initiated the support ticket and will keep you updated on what it reveals.
>
> How have you been otherwise?

I'm thrilled to give him an update on how I've been. I was a mess on Saturday night—so much so that he offered his costly therapy services. But life has taken a significant turn in my favor, and I want him to know it.

> 3:07 PM

> I'm doing great, Ethan—thanks for
> asking! Tony and I have decided to work
> things out. Best of luck in finding and
> meeting your true match. I hope there's
> a special person out there for you—you
> deserve it!

After hitting *Send*, a sense of closure washes over me. Ethan was kind and supportive, even if he wasn't meant to be my quantum match, and it feels good to leave things on a hopeful, positive note.

Then, my phone vibrates again.

Ethan Clarendon: 3:08 PM

So, Tony's no longer with his match?

A quick, shallow breath escapes me as I lower my phone, glancing around with sudden hyper-awareness of my surroundings. Pedestrians move with me on the MWT and on the adjacent track heading in the opposite direction, their steady pace contrasting with my unsettled state.

A strange discomfort settles over me. I don't want to say too much—or too little. I don't want Ethan to judge me or nudge me into rethinking my pact with Tony.

Somehow, I doubt Ethan has ever fallen in love the way Tony and I have. He couldn't possibly understand what this feels like, and no amount of psychotherapy could ever illuminate it for him.

Fueled by this conviction, I'm ready to reply.

3:11 PM

> No, but it's complicated. He still loves
> me. We met for lunch today, and he
> confirmed it.

After hitting send, a rush of unfinished thoughts lingers. Part of me wants to tell Ethan more, to explain the rare beauty of meeting someone by chance, falling in love, and building a life together; how it's a gift that doesn't come to everyone. But it had for Tony and me.

I want to say, *so please, Ethan, stop. Let it be. Let us have the chance to repair what was never broken until something tried to convince us it was.*

His silence stretches out with an unsettling weight, gnawing at my fragile optimism. It's strange—almost eerie—how the absence of a reply leaves me restless, doubting the words I just sent.

Just as I consider putting my phone away, the screen flickers. Three small dots appear, dancing in anticipation.

And then, he replies.

> Ethan Clarendon: 3:15 PM

> > I understand. My offer from Saturday
> > still stands—if you ever need support,
> > I'm here, free of charge. Here's my
> > personal number: 276-566-1333.
> > Wishing you all the best.

I look up, gazing forward without truly seeing anything, though my stop comes into view not too far ahead. I don't want to say anything else to him, especially not *thank you.*

Why do I feel like he's patronizing me? He says he *understands*, but I don't believe him. He doesn't know the connection between Tony and me. He's a therapist, not some all-knowing force.

Tucking my phone back into my coat pocket, I refocus on reaching my stop, finishing my workday, and heading home.

And tonight, I'll dream about the future Tony and I will reclaim together. Come hell or high water, we *will* reclaim it.

THURSDAY, OCTOBER 29, 2099

CHAPTER TWELVE

M onday afternoon, my whole body felt lighter. Smiling came easily, and during my last class, I could tell my students were truly engaged, asking thoughtful questions. For the first time in a long while, I felt on fire as a lecturer.

But today? I'm running on fumes. Tony hasn't answered any of my texts—not even the quick, sweet notes about how much I love and miss him. *It's fine.* At least he knows how I feel.

The day started rough and only got worse. I was seventeen minutes late to my 9:00 a.m. lecture, apologizing so much that my stomach twisted with guilt. But that wasn't the worst of it. Nearly an hour in, a student raised her hand and asked how the new material connected to the rest of the course. My heart sank. I'd been lecturing from the wrong outline. Embarrassed, I dismissed them early. The look in their eyes was hard to ignore—the way they glanced at each other, eyebrows raised in silent, mutual pity.

Last night, I did it again. I watched them.

Wedged between the hedges, heart hammering, time stood still as I peered through those massive, exhibitionist windows. Tony's house is designed to showcase every corner, every step within its walls.

Tanya was there, gliding through the hallways, up and down the stairs in luxurious-looking pajamas. She's definitely living there. She moved as if basking in the spotlight of what was once my life. Her phone was glued to her hand; she's always on that damn phone. My fingers gripped the coarse branches so hard I didn't notice a sprig pricking my skin—not enough to draw blood but enough to sting.

And then Tony appeared, still in his suit—the one he obviously wore to the office. They kissed, their lips lingering in a way that felt endless. He lifted her off the floor, her legs wrapping around his waist as he carried her out of view, mouths still locked together.

They went to make love.

My body trembled, a sharp breath escaping me as I beat back the urge to break down and cry.

With a bit of distance now, I know I should've left, spared myself the agony. But I didn't. I stayed, breath held, eyes glued to every flicker of movement, waiting for them to reappear. And they did—Tony, freshly dressed, composed as ever, and Tanya, draped in a faux fur coat, heels clicking as she carried a cocktail purse.

In a hurry, they exited their stage. In the driveway, Tony's silver Zenith Summit SUV pulled up out of the underground four-car garage, its headlights slicing through the night.

I kept my gaze fixed on them as the gate opened and the taillights of Tony's SUV disappeared around the corner. Slowly, I turned my focus back to the house. As usual, within moments, the lights shut off, leaving only the few that stayed on when no one was home.

Gnawing nervously on my lower lip, I ran through a list of reasons why Tony and Tanya seemed so relaxed, so content in this life they were sharing.

Alright, so they have a physical connection—a strong one, clearly. In the beginning, Tony and I had that too, a spark so intense we couldn't keep our hands off each other. Anywhere, all the time. But then, we settled into something deeper, a kind of comfort they probably haven't reached yet. Maybe they're still riding the high of that initial spark.

And maybe they like going out more than staying in. Tony loves being the center of attention, and I wouldn't be surprised if Tanya did too. That could be a source of contention between them. Unlike her, I always enjoyed letting him take the spotlight, watching him shine.

Maybe last night was just a fun night, nothing more. But still, the urge to know more gnawed at me.

All I had to do was step out of the hedges and into the yard. Pulling up the security system app on my phone, I saw that Tony hadn't armed the system, as usual. The temptation to slip inside my old home was overwhelming. To search for some kind of clue about his intentions. To find out how close he was to making a decision.

A sharp buzz jolts me back to reality, and my desk cube lights up with a notification. Ray, the assistant to my department head, Lena Chest, is calling. Seeing her name on the ID plate sends a knot forming in my stomach. A call at this time of day is rarely a good sign.

Forcing a steady breath, I tap the answer button. "Hello?" My voice comes out cautious, tense.

"Sienna?" Ray's voice is bright and friendly, putting me somewhat at ease.

"Yes?"

"Lena would like to see you in her office."

I glance at the time on the cube. Unfortunately, I have plenty of time before my next class. "Now?"

"Yes, now."

CHAPTER THIRTEEN

I've been sitting in this itchy wool armchair for several minutes, enduring Lena's unfiltered rundown of my faults. She didn't offer coffee, didn't ease in with small talk—just dove straight into the charges. And the worst part? I have no defense. Everything she's saying is true.

Yes, I've been late returning term papers. Yes, my passion for teaching has dwindled—Monday afternoon, after lunch with Tony, being the lone exception I could even mention.

Lena stops speaking, and the sudden silence jars me. Two realizations hit me at once: how distant her voice had sounded, and that my gaze had wandered to her bookcase, unfocused, instead of on her. My face warms as I blink myself back to the present.

Now that I'm paying attention, I notice Lena watching me intently, her expression a mix of concern and something uncomfortably close to pity.

She shifts in her oversized executive chair, the vast seat making her petite frame seem even smaller. With practiced calm, she entwines her fingers and leans back against the leather, her gaze steady on me.

"The students have reported this because many of them are worried, Sienna," she says, her voice softening. "And frankly, so am I. You were one of the stars of the department. Students once said they signed up for your class because you were engaging, interesting—a breath of fresh air."

I swallow hard, the familiar ache in my chest rising again. What once felt like compliments now linger in the air as quiet accusations, each one a stark reminder of a version of myself I can barely recognize.

My lips press tighter with each passing second. I find myself utterly lost for words.

"How's everything at home?" Lena asks gently, a soft smile tugging at her lips, as though willing me into a better state of mind. "Are you and that handsome husband of yours still in the honeymoon phase?"

My eyes start to water as I meet her gaze. She doesn't know. None of my colleagues know about the separation—the endless turmoil that has consumed my life. The warm, unexpected tears streaming down my face catch me off guard. I thought I was holding it together better than this.

"Oh, Sienna, no..." Lena's voice is soft, filled with concern. In an instant, she's reaching for the tissue box perched on the corner of her desk. She hands it to me, her expression flooded with sympathy.

"We're not together," I manage, sniffing, trying to sound strong, unaffected. It's not working. Each word feels like it's exposing more than I intend. "It's the… the band," I add, my voice faltering. "The YPM band."

Lena's hand flies to her mouth, her expression a mixture of shock and dismay. "Oh no."

I nod, quick and sharp, the details spilling out like accusations as I recount the night Tony presented the bands to me. He made them feel like a gift, a celebration —something I was supposed to cherish. Maybe that's why I accepted it so easily, I think bitterly now.

I tell Lena about the rush of it all: how Tony found his match almost instantly, how I convinced myself it was just a scam, that our love would see us through. I had always believed in our love story—a girl caught on the hamster wheel of life, never dreaming of Prince Charming, but then finding one. A man who fit that image in every way. A man I loved madly. I truly thought we'd live happily ever after.

Her face crumples in sympathy. "And you separated in August?"

"Yes," I reply, my voice shaky but controlled.

"What a…" She rubs her temple, clearly distressed by my story. Her reaction brings an unexpected sense of relief, as though her being upset is a form of validation. Normally, I'd temper my words about Tony, painting him in a more reasonable light. But after last night— after seeing them together—I let myself absorb her sympathy, unfiltered and unrestrained.

"I'm so sorry, Sienna. That explains… well, it

explains a lot. But still..." Her lips press together, the words perched on the tip of her tongue. She hesitates, reluctant to say what's coming next.

My heart pounds in my throat, each second stretching unbearably as I wait for whatever penalty she's about to pass down.

"We had a department meeting and decided it would be best to absorb all your classes within the faculty next quarter."

I blink, the words hanging between us as I try to piece together what she's saying. I'd thought I was in trouble for this morning's mistake—teaching the wrong material to my students. But this decision? It's from the regular faculty meeting held Tuesday, the one lecturers aren't invited to.

My mix-up today wasn't the cause; it was just confirmation that they've made the right decision.

"You mean... I'm fired?" The question slips out in a voice so quiet, I barely hear it myself.

Lena's gaze softens, studying my face in silence, as if searching for something—some sign that I understand, that I'm ready to let go. "Oh, Sienna," she murmurs, her eyes filled with pity. "Maybe it's time for you to blaze another trail. You passed the bar; you could easily work as a lawyer."

I shake my head, my gaze drifting as I repel the thought of moving on, of taking another step in life without Tony. He's always nudged me toward practicing law, urging me to aim higher. *Do better,* he'd say, echoing words I've heard his mother say to him countless times.

But I don't have the drive to *do better* right now. And come next year, I'll be unemployed.

I need Tony.

Maybe this is fate working in my favor. I'll talk to him, see what he says.

"Maybe," I say, merely pacifying her.

"That damn YPM has destroyed more marriages than a mistress," Lena mutters, grimacing. Then, with a hint of concern, she asks, "Do you have someone to talk to about it?"

I resist the urge to roll my eyes. "Like a therapist?" The word feels heavy on my tongue, and frankly, I'm tired of the endless suggestions to see one.

"I meant family, friends…" she clarifies.

"Oh." I exhale, a little relieved we're not diving into the therapist conversation again. But the answer remains the same. "No, not really."

Suddenly, Lena abruptly scoots to the edge of her chair. "What are you doing tonight?"

"Huh?" I blink, caught off guard by her sudden question.

"Would you like to join me and Leo for dinner?" she offers, her voice warm and inviting. "We're making braised short ribs—delicious, comforting, real comfort food." Her eyebrows lift in a coaxing gesture.

The invitation surprises me. I think of my usual evening routine: a sandwich, obsessively watching Tony's security feed, texting him over and over, calling only to hear his voicemail, then lying in bed—too hurt, too ignored, and too confused to find any rest.

Do I want another night of that?

Forcing a small smile, I nod. "Sure, I'd like that."

Lena's face lights up. "Good. Seven o'clock? Just bring yourself, okay?"

I nod again, feeling an odd but welcome sense of relief. For once, I've chosen to break the cycle and take a step toward something—anything—different.

CHAPTER FOURTEEN

TONY

Heavy rain has come to the Southland, hammering the windows of this upscale corporate high-rise in a rhythmic drone. Everyone's tempted to leave early, myself included, but finally connecting with James has kept me rooted. I'm convinced he's been dodging me—unprofessional and outright disrespectful, especially given that I'm his boss. Talented as he is, I can't let him test my authority this way.

A light knock breaks through the rain's lull. It's him —I'd recognize that timid, almost apologetic tapping anywhere. His knocking alone tells me he's wary. While I should dial down the intensity, I need him to understand he's crossed a line.

"Come in," I call, letting a bit of a lion's roar slip into my tone.

The door cracks open, and James, a slender man in his early thirties, fragile through and through, leans halfway across the threshold. "I heard you wanted to talk to me," he says.

I rise, easily towering over him. The height difference only enhances my sense of authority. "Close it," I say firmly.

James hesitates, then steps fully into the room, easing the door shut with a quiet click. "How can I help you?"

"Sit." I gesture toward the sofas.

He perches on the edge of the cushion as if poised to bolt. I lean back against my desk, arms crossed. "It seems we have a problem."

"A problem with what?"

His timidity is starting to wear on me. My gaze shifts through the glass wall that separates my office from the floor full of cubicles, where project assistants are hard at work. Julie, my executive assistant, is typing steadily on the deliverables report for five projects I assigned her. Look at her—focused, unruffled, handling everything with ease. She's not scared of me. So why is James acting like I'm some kind of monster?

"The YPM bands," I say, shifting my focus back to him.

A flash of panic crosses his face, momentarily baffling me. Is it genuine or just another act? I can never quite tell. Sometimes, I wonder if his timidity is more strategy than personality—a deliberate tactic to deflect or evade.

"What about the YPM bands?" he asks, his voice nearly drowned out by the relentless patter of rain against the windows.

After lunch with Sienna, I checked my account. The

box—the one confirming that consenting couples have received counseling from a licensed family and marriage therapist—was left unchecked. I don't have the authority to change it now, not at this juncture. The only reason my account and Sienna's haven't been flagged for review is likely due to the unconventional way I brought them online and active in the first place.

But I need that box checked on both accounts.

I can't do it myself. The only person who can is sitting right in front of me.

It's simple, really: check a box on two Quantum Matching accounts. That's it. *What's the big deal?*

Of course, it's wrong. It could get both of us fired. And yet, I have no other option. I have to convince James to do it, even as his wary gaze locks onto me like I'm about to club him with a bat. He's making it clear that this won't be easy.

"Did you know you had to check the box saying Sienna and I saw a therapist before activating our bands?" I ask, though I already know the answer.

"No," he replies, shaking his head adamantly. "Did you?"

I pin him with a look I know he doesn't like, rubbing the stubble on my jaw as I realize I didn't shave this morning. Last night was rough—I barely slept after making love to Tanya with a fervor that felt like a desperate bid to hold our entire relationship together. Three hours of sleep, max. Between that and the incessant rain, I'm itching to get home. But this unchecked box is gnawing at me, and I know someone could end up in serious trouble over it.

I pause, holding back the urge to make a smart-ass comment. If I hadn't seen it with my own eyes, I'd sometimes doubt how brilliant James is. He's so pragmatic that he can't strategize outside the box. I mean, seriously—would I be asking him about the boxes if I'd known to check them in the first place?

I plaster on a huge smile, all teeth, ready for my next approach.

"It's probably just a simple box to tick, right?"

James knows exactly what I'm implying, but neither of us can afford for me to say it outright.

"I don't know."

"You should probably check, though," I say, light, almost breezy. "And if it *is* just a box… go ahead and tick it."

James's brows knit together as he processes my meaning, the lines across his forehead deepening the closer he gets to catching on.

"What are you asking me to do?" he finally asks, his voice barely audible.

I don't answer directly, just narrow my eyes, letting the silence convey what I can't say aloud.

A sudden knock on the window startles both of us, breaking the intense eye contact. My head snaps up to see Sara standing in the hallway, waving with an expectant grin.

"Shit," I mutter under my breath, forcing a smile as I wave back. She points to the door, silently asking if she can come in.

CHAPTER FIFTEEN

TONY

James is on his feet the moment Sara steps into the room. "Good then," he mutters, his voice tight, like he's just taken a punch to the gut.

Despite her small frame, Sara commands the doorway with ease, her presence blocking his path. Her sharp, unwavering attention locks onto him. "Hey, James," she says casually, though there's a deliberate edge to her tone, her gaze flickering over him in an assessing way.

"Hi, Sara." His voice is low, barely audible, and he doesn't quite meet her eyes. His discomfort is written all over him—too plainly, in my opinion. If he keeps wearing his unease like this, it's only a matter of time before someone picks up on it. Maybe not Sara, but someone sharper. And if they do, it could lead straight back to me.

Sara's eyes narrow slightly, as if trying to parse the tension hanging in the air. Her attention shifts to me, lingering for a beat. "Great dinner the other night," she says.

I don't want to talk about that dinner, especially not with James here.

"Alexander had a great time," Sara adds casually.

"Alexander Creston?" James blurts out, suddenly and miraculously springing to life.

It's a battle to stay composed. All this time, he's been acting like a mute, and *this* is what gets him to talk? Alexander Creston?

Shit. I need to say something—anything—to cut this off before it spins completely out of control.

"You know of him?" Sara asks, jumping in before I can suggest James leave.

James swipes his palms down his slacks, clearly uncomfortable. "Yeah, well. I've heard of him."

"Thanks for stopping by, James. We'll finish up later," I interject, slicing the conversation clean off before it can go further.

James nods almost too eagerly and barely glances at Sara as he slips past her and out the door.

My mind spins as Sara turns to watch him leave, her curiosity visibly piqued.

"What's with him?" she asks, her eyes narrowing at the door as if trying to solve a riddle.

The quickest way to get her moving on and out of my office is to ignore the question, so I say nothing.

"I think he has a crush on me," she declares confidently, as if her conclusion is obvious.

"Maybe that's it," I reply, hoping this will satisfy her enough to drop the subject.

Instead of leaving, Sara settles onto the couch.

"By the way, I've been wondering—how's Sienna?"

Still leaning against the front of my desk, I force my fingers to stop tapping the surface. Abruptly, I straighten up.

"She's fine," I reply curtly. Why the hell is she asking about Sienna?

"I've always liked her. She's elegant, you know. Is she with her match too?"

"Yes," I say, walking to my desk chair and settling into it, though unease lingers in my chest.

"So, the two of you are happily in love with other people?"

"Yes."

"Hmm..." she hums, thoughtful. "You just got married on New Year's Day—and *voilà*, your YPM match changed everything?"

My lips press tight, holding back the urge to snap, *"Why are you in my office asking these questions?"*

"I mean," she continues, her gaze drifting thoughtfully, "I like Alexander. A lot. He's a great guy, easily anyone's dream partner."

Then it comes—the telltale moment. Her lips part, her eyes widening just slightly.

"But..." She sighs, her voice softening. "I'm not in love with him. He's wonderful, but... something's missing. And we're supposed to have this eternal bond. Don't you and Tanya have that?"

"Yeah." I'm done with this conversation.

Checking my watch, I stand. "Sorry to hear that," I

say, my tone clipped. "But I have a meeting. Is there anything else you need?"

"Oh..." She looks startled, as if she didn't expect our little heart-to-heart to end so abruptly. "Well, yes." Rising to her feet, she smooths her dress. "I wanted to send a digital invitation for the New Year's Eve celebration to Tanya. We exchanged numbers once, but I must've deleted it. Could you—"

"Send it to me," I cut in, already striding across the office to grab my coat. I'll catch up with James tomorrow. I'm going home.

"But the invitation is designed to create a personal experience for each—"

"Sara. She'll be fine." My coat slips over my shoulders, and I grab my keys from my pocket. "I have to go now, or I'll be late."

"Oh," she says, stunned.

I open the door, standing aside as a silent cue for her to exit. Her lips press into a thin line, and she shakes her head slightly, clearly disappointed with the abrupt ending.

I don't care. I should care, but I don't.

"Goodbye, Sara." My voice is colder than I intended.

She blinks, clearly taken aback. Then, almost unthinkingly, she murmurs, "Goodbye."

Thankfully, she doesn't say anything else. She heads off in the opposite direction, looking distracted.

As I make my way to the elevators, eager to escape to the parking garage, I pull out my phone and tap out a quick text to James.

We're not done, I write, then pause.

I delete it. I have to be careful about what I say to him.

And then it comes to mind.

> 3:23 P.M.
>
> We're not done ✓. Do it.

There. That should do the trick.

CHAPTER SIXTEEN

R ain changes everything. People slow down, plans get scrapped, and most folks stay indoors. I'd almost canceled tonight's dinner with Lena and her husband, Leo, but the thought of spending another night alone in my apartment stopped me. I could already picture it—staring at my phone, waiting for something that would never come. The thought gnawed at me, leaving no room for the urge to waste away in solitude.

That's why I find myself here, making my way to Lena's home. She and Leo live in one of the oldest neighborhoods in a city transformed during the 2070s to fit the "smart-living" vision. The infrastructure is seam-less—accessible Swift railways, MWT walkways connecting schools, shops, hospitals, and even the beaches.

Driving these days is reserved for people with nothing better to do or those eager to show off a sleek car. Tony would definitely fall into the latter category, flaunting his car at every opportunity.

The bitter thoughts about him have been simmering for weeks, and since Lena told me I'd effectively lost my job, they've only worsened.

I rode the Swift from Century City to the coastal end of the city. It took less than ten minutes, but somehow, it was enough time to sink deep into vexing thoughts that wouldn't leave me alone. They are relentless, swirling constantly, and I'm convinced the only thing that could stop them is going back to my old life, back to Tony.

With a bright yellow umbrella ballooned above me, I walk up the cobblestone pathway, bordered by a perfectly manicured lawn. Lena's house is painted a soft green, its stucco exterior charmingly out of place in the sleek, modern cityscape.

Stopping at the decorative iron gate, I ring the doorbell and listen to the gentle chime echo behind the tall mahogany double doors. They're truly beautiful—so timeless, so inviting.

One of the doors swings open, and Lena's face lights up. "You made it!"

As I step inside, the comforting aroma of dinner fills the air. "I wasn't going to let a little rain get the best of me," I say, echoing the inside joke every Californian understands.

Laughing, Lena collects my damp coat and umbrella, disappearing briefly to hang them in the dry box. "Smell those ribs? They came out perfectly. The meat is falling off the bone," she calls from down the hall.

"Ooh. Can't wait to partake!" I reply, lingering in the entryway just long enough to catch my reflection in the large, gold-framed mirror nearby.

I pause, almost startled. The person staring back at me looks unfamiliar. My jeans hang loose, as if they're two sizes too big, and my eggplant-purple cashmere sweater swallows me whole. My cheeks are hollow, my eyes wide, my skin pallid. I look... faded.

Lena reappears, standing in the doorway, watching me with gentle curiosity. "Shall we head to the den?" she asks, and I wonder how long she's been there, silently witnessing my stunned reaction to my own reflection.

CHAPTER SEVENTEEN

I can't remember the last time I ate this well—maybe it was last Saturday's steak at Urban Ember. Ethan was right; it was absolutely delicious. But seeing myself in the mirror earlier today, I realized I need to eat more. That's why tonight, I've cleared everything on my plate, plus dessert. Now, we're winding down with coffee. I love the way this feels—lounging in their comfortable den, surrounded by warmth. There's a quiet satisfaction in the air, an unspoken contentment that feels rare and precious.

We haven't touched on the topic of my classes being absorbed by the department, or why it happened. I thought for sure Lena would carve out some time to mention it. In a way, I'm glad she hasn't. What more could she say? I don't even know why I half-expected her to bring it up. Maybe it's because we're having such a lovely time tonight—after she actually fired me earlier today.

Come to think of it, it's the most genuine act

anyone's ever bestowed upon me. *I fired you, now let's break bread and really get to know each other better!*

The conversation shifts to Leo and Lena's two sons, Asa and Chat. Both are away at university but will be home soon for the holidays. Asa, the younger, is studying archaeology with dreams of leading excavations in overlooked countries. Chat, the older, is delving into chemistry and geology. Their futures sound full of promise and adventure—worlds apart from mine.

For a fleeting moment, I wonder if my relentless pursuit of Tony could ever bring me the kind of satisfaction their sons seem destined for. But instead of voicing my thoughts, I ask Lena and Leo how they met. I admire their bond—it seems so grounded, so enduring. They have the life I once thought my marriage would give me.

"We were set up on a blind date by my cousin Sheila," Leo says, smiling at the memory. "Sheila met Lena at a conference on ethics and law."

"She was convinced we'd be perfect for each other," Lena adds, rolling her eyes. "She said we had the same deadpan humor and no-nonsense approach to life. Which struck me as odd, considering I don't have deadpan humor."

She laughs lightly, glancing at Leo. "When we met, there was a spark, sure—but nothing like fireworks. Wouldn't you agree?"

Leo scratches his temple thoughtfully, as though searching for the right words. "Well, yeah—because you seemed bored."

"That's because I was starving, and you took me to eat dim sum," Lena deadpans.

"You should've seen her devour those dumplings," Leo counters, his tone equally deadpan.

I laugh, watching as they effortlessly prove Leo's cousin right. They truly are a perfect fit.

"Can I ask you something?" I say, observing the warmth between them. "Have you two ever considered the YPM band?"

"No," they reply in unison, sharing a quick, knowing smile.

"Never," Lena adds, her voice firm but fond. "I'm sure there's some *perfect* person out there for me, but Leo is my imperfect perfect choice."

My heart swells as they reach across the table to clasp hands. No YPM band needed to forge that bond—it's pure, chosen, and theirs.

"What about you and Tony?" Lena asks, her eyes warm but curious. "How did you two meet?"

My heart flutters, memories swelling up as if they happened only yesterday. I drift back to that first moment on Wilshire Boulevard, when Tony and I locked eyes—he was exiting Roast Coffee, and I was entering.

"There were fireworks at first sight," I admit, warmth rushing to my face. "He felt them too. You were at our wedding—you saw how magical we were together."

I let the words flow, spilling memories of those early days—the dancing, the hiking, our spontaneous week on Catalina. "We lived off sex and room service," I say, letting the memory sweep me away for a moment. "No one's ever made me feel so cherished, so adored, as Tony."

A pause settles over the room, grounding me back to the present. Leo's lips press together as he studies the table, his expression unreadable. Lena, however, meets my gaze with a knowing look—one that makes me feel exposed, as if she wants to say something but is holding back.

"I know how it might sound," I add quickly, trying to dispel any doubts hanging in the air. "I've dated my share of frogs. But Tony loves me. It's this technology, I'm convinced of it. It's like… mind control. The YPM band affects the brain. I've read about it online—accounts from people who've had the same experience." And, deep down, I truly believe those stories.

"May I ask you something?" Leo's voice is soft, almost slipping under the conversation like a whisper through a crack in the door.

I stiffen, wary but unwilling to deny him. "Sure."

"Forget what he's feeling, thinking, or experiencing. What he's offering in the way of love, respect even—is that enough for you?"

I open my mouth, but no words come. Instead, I pause, taking an unexpected emotional inventory. His question feels like a double-edged sword—a trap. If I answer "yes," I'm justifying whatever scraps I've been handed. If I answer "no," I'm admitting to a lack I don't want to face.

"No need to answer that, Sienna," Lena interjects, her gaze sweeping over Leo, who seems content to leave the question lingering. "At least not now," she adds, her tone maddeningly gentle. "Maybe when you're alone and ready to make some difficult decisions."

Anger flares inside me, hot and unrelenting, though I keep it tightly in check. A polite smile stretches across my face—cordial, reserved. After all, Lena is still my boss. But how dare they? Is this why she invited me over? To dissect my marriage?

"Absolutely," I reply, my voice smooth, though it takes effort.

After a few moments of strained, polite conversation, I fake a yawn and thank them for dinner. There's a quick round of hugs and goodbyes, but as I step out the door, a storm brews within me.

I'm furious, wounded, hopeless—and yet, more determined than ever to win my husband back.

THURSDAY, NOVEMBER 12, 2099

CHAPTER EIGHTEEN

TONY

The buzz of my phone slices through the heavy silence hanging in the bedroom.

"Could you please turn that thing off?" Tanya sighs, her exasperation sharp and unmistakable.

It's late afternoon, and she's in bed beside me, naked, her head nestled into the pillow. We both called in sick today. I should be at the office, keeping an eye on things, but this morning was one of those mornings—I couldn't bring myself to leave her body. She's like an addiction, one I wish I didn't have. Needing her this much makes me weak, vulnerable. No woman has ever held this kind of power over me. She could break me if she wanted, and that's why I tread carefully with Tanya.

There's something about her, something dark and consuming. She's shaky ground, and yet somehow, I'm welded to it. To her.

Now that she's pointed it out, the familiar itch to check my phone returns. Reaching over, I see Sienna's name flashing across the screen. She's been texting me constantly—five or six times a day. The messages are always the same: *"I love you,"* or *"I'm patient."*

I can't bring myself to answer. Her desperation irritates me, even a bit off-putting. But as much as I'd like to shut it down completely, part of me holds back. I'm the one who left her in limbo, the asshole who pulled the plug on everything. Sienna is a good person, and she doesn't deserve the hammer brought down all the way.

I glance at Tanya, noting how she's gripping the covers tightly under her arm, her back rigid, shoulders tense. She's clearly upset that I looked at my phone.

"Who is it?" she asks, her irritation poorly masked.

"It's James," I say, the lie slipping out without hesitation.

Just in case she flips over to catch a glimpse of my screen, I hop out of bed. Sienna would never try something like that—she always respected my space, my privacy. But Tanya? I know better.

As I read Sienna's latest message, I rub a hand over my chest. The ache settles in, sharp and relentless, as though my heart is clenched tight in a fist.

> Sienna: 4:39 PM
>
> My false match submitted a help ticket to check for errors. What's the best way to handle this?

SHE WONDERS WHETHER SHE SHOULD HOLD OUT UNTIL I make up my mind about us, or meet whoever the system claims is her true match once the error is resolved. I don't even know what the hell she's talking about. But now, with a help ticket flagged under her name, it poses a whole new problem for me.

Thinking quickly, I start typing.

> 4:42 PM
>
> What's the name of the guy you were mistakenly matched with?

Tanya flips over, her gaze sharp. "What are you doing?"

Damn it. I'm sitting here, waiting on pins and needles for Sienna's reply. I need that name now. And I know I won't have to wait long—Sienna's always waiting to hear from me. I like it that way.

"James is having an issue with one of the accounts," I reply, feigning nonchalance.

Tanya groans, flipping onto her back. Her smooth, toned body distracts me instantly, her chest rising and falling in a way that almost makes me forget the whole mess I'm tangled in. *Almost.*

And then—finally—my phone vibrates, the screen lighting up with the notification.

> Sienna: 4:43 PM
>
> Ethan.

I clench my jaw, frustration tightening like a vice. *Come on, Sienna,* I want to shout. *Think! Give me a first and last name!*

> 4:44 PM
>
> Does he have a last name?

"Get over here already," Tanya says, her hip curled and raised seductively.

I'm beyond ready for Tanya—for her body, a promise I'm seconds away from keeping. But first…

> Sienna: 4:45 PM
>
> Cranston

"Give me a few more seconds," I say, grinning as I fire off another message to James. He'd better not ignore me this time—he can't afford to. This help desk ticket has raised the stakes, escalating everything to a whole new level. And now, his ass is on the line far more than mine.

> 4:46 PM
>
> Her match submitted a help ticket.
> Ethan Cranston.

Satisfied, I delete all traces of my conversation with Sienna before showing Tanya my screen, filled with messages to James—three from earlier and the latest one.

"See?" I say. "Work."

Her eyes scan the screen with that familiar inquisitive glint. That's Tanya—never one to miss a detail. But my phone is just far enough away for her to miss the specifics of what I've written. She's content not seeing Sienna's name anywhere. Leaning back with a sly smile, her gaze locks onto mine, luring me in."Well then," she purrs, her voice dripping with invitation, "come over here and work on me."

Setting my phone on the nightstand, I grin, both satisfied and relieved. And then, I make her wish, my command.

MONDAY, NOVEMBER 16, 2099

CHAPTER NINETEEN

Tony stopped answering my texts the moment I sent him Ethan's last name. To salvage what little dignity I have left, I stopped messaging him too. But now my fingernails are chewed to the quick, and I can't count my hours of sleep over the past four nights on two hands. I'm spiraling, my mind assaulted by relentless questions: *Why did Tony want Ethan's last name? Is he playing me? Hiding something?* Each time I come close to answering, I pull back, the uncertainty gnawing at my sanity.

My energy is drained, and my work is suffering. At least the revised divorce papers arrived. If I don't respond by December 30th, the divorce will go through automatically. When I opened the envelope, I stared at the papers, and for just a second, I thought, *Why am I letting him pull my strings?* I'm the lawyer. *I* should be steering this process.

We were married less than a year, but long enough for me to push for more than what he's offering. *Why did*

I move out of the house anyway? I should've stayed. Sure, Tony wouldn't have been happy, but at least I would've been fighting for what I wanted. Instead, I feel like I'm shadowboxing, swinging at air while he moves further out of reach. Now, I've hit rock bottom—or maybe I'm still spiraling toward it.

I can't get comfortable in my own skin. Today, I canceled my classes; my throat aches, my head pounds, and every joint feels twisted out of place. I pace my apartment, craving coffee but too restless to stop and make it. I need answers. *Now.*

Checking my phone, I see it's 11:37 a.m. Tony could be at Roast, the coffee shop where we first met. If he goes, this is around the time he likes to show up. Before and after we were married, I used to rearrange my breaks and shuffle my schedule just to "accidentally" run into him there. Seeing him in the middle of the day always felt like a jolt of energy, a little electric surge that carried me through. I loved knowing that *little ole me* had managed to capture the attention of a man so seemingly perfect. I never stopped wondering how I'd gotten so lucky.

That need for him hasn't faded. It burns as strongly now as it did then.

I stop pacing, rush to my bedroom, and dive into the closet, grabbing the first outfit I can find: jeans, a sweatshirt, socks, and sneakers. It doesn't look cold outside, but I grab my coat just in case. Then I catch a whiff of myself. *Shit.* I haven't showered in two days, and the sharp, pungent scent rising from my armpits is unmistakably stress sweat. Dashing to the bathroom, I swipe on deodorant, praying it'll suffice.

Every passing second feels like a lifetime. The longer I take, the greater the risk of missing him. Impatiently, I toss the deodorant onto the counter, grab my purse, and head out. My stride is brisk, purposeful, driven by urgency. When I finally settle into a seat on the Swift, a wave of relief washes over me. The ride to the coffee shop is only seven minutes, and at this hour, there will barely be any stops.

CHAPTER TWENTY

I order a house coffee, black, and a fresh strawberry croissant. After paying, I linger near the counter, waiting for my order before settling into a nook against the wall. From here, I can see everyone who enters. My eyes scan face after face, hoping to catch sight of him.

"Sienna?"

I jump, startled, and look up at a woman standing at the edge of my table. She looks familiar, but I can't quite place her.

"It's me, Sara. I'm Tony's work colleague."

Sara watches me with an oddly sympathetic expression, speaking as though I'm something fragile. At least, that's how it feels. I could be wrong.

Now that she's explained herself, her face clicks into place. We'd had a long conversation at last year's company Christmas party. Tony and I had been the center of attention, with everyone congratulating us on our upcoming wedding. After introducing me around and basking in the praise, Tony left to mingle on his own. I spent most of the night rooted in a chair by myself until I noticed Sara seated at the next table. She smiled, and I smiled back.

"Good food," she'd said, nibbling on pastry puffs.

I chuckled, and she came over. We introduced ourselves.

Conversation with Sara had been easy. We talked about everything. I confessed my occasional regret over studying law, admitting it felt too late to change paths.

"It's never too late," she'd said in a lighthearted, musical way. Her optimism felt comforting and, at the same time, painfully out of reach. But I loved our talk, which drifted from her tips for making the perfect chicken and dumplings to my fascination with etymology and how language reveals truths buried by power.

When I shared thoughts like that with Tony, he'd brush them off. "Who cares about that? We're here now. Figure out how to get ahead with things as they are."

But Sara had listened intently, murmuring, "How fascinating," and meaning it.

Then Tony came to collect me. I still remember his quiet, disparaging comments about Sara afterward—calling her "loony" and "unserious," hinting she didn't belong in their department. After that night, I'd often found myself wondering about her, seeing her as a potential friend I could never have. Tony had a way of subtly discouraging me from getting close to anyone associated with him—friends, family, even work colleagues.

"Oh, hi, Sara," I finally manage to say, my focus splintered between her and the steady stream of people coming through the door.

"How are you?" she asks, chipper as ever.

"Have you seen Tony?" I blurt out, desperation spilling into my voice before I can stop it.

She crosses her arms, settling in as though for a friendly chat, but her words hit like a wrecking ball. "Tony and Tanya are on a mini-vacay. To celebrate their engagement, I believe."

My jaw drops. The shock lands like a slap, leaving me momentarily breathless. Sara notices, which might be why she adds, "But...you found your match too, right?"

The world tilts, spinning away from me. I feel rootless, adrift. My heart seems to have fallen out of its chamber, but there's no pain in my chest—just a numb urgency propelling me to leave.

"Sorry, Sara, but I have to go," I say, grabbing my purse from the back of the chair.

I don't wait for her reply. I'm already moving, stepping out onto the bustling street. A cool breeze rushes up the avenue, slapping my face with a jolt of clarity I refuse to acknowledge.

I need answers about Tony and Tanya—more than the scraps Sara has offered.

As I walk briskly, barely aware of where my feet are taking me, a hot wave of resentment surges through me.

It's unfair, I know. Sara was only trying to be kind. Still, in this moment, as my world cracks open, I can't stop myself from despising her—and, if I'm honest, everything else around me.

CHAPTER TWENTY-ONE

Frustration courses through me as I slip into the hedges surrounding Tony's house—the house that should still be ours. I hate having to sneak around like this, moving covertly, but it's always manageable. People in LA disappear into their homes like they're fading from reality. Tony and I used to do the same. In a way, that makes this feel almost too easy.

Still, it gnaws at me that I can't just stroll through the front gate like I belong here, like I still have a place in his life. If Tony were to check the livestream of his security cameras right now, he'd see me crossing the perfectly manicured lawn, stepping up the imperial sheet-rock stairs to the porch. The alarm would've gone off too—if I hadn't disarmed the system during my ride over.

The fact that Tony hasn't changed the passcode burrows under my skin, a haunting thread I keep pulling at, desperate to believe it means he's still open to me somehow. But that belief feels thinner, hollower with each passing second, leaving behind an ache that's almost unbearable. Maybe he thinks of me like he does Sara—someone to toy with, a puppet he assumes isn't strong or clever enough to take control.

But look, Tony. Here I am. Capable, determined, standing inside *our* house while you're off on a "mini-vacay."

The scent hits me first—a floral perfume, cloying and insistent, woven into the air like Tanya's signature. Beneath it, though, is *his* scent, sharp and familiar, threading its way through my senses and tightening my chest. It's bittersweet, so close and yet painfully out of reach, flooding me with memories I'm not ready to let go of.

Gone are Tony's prized white leather Moon Cloud sectionals by Chas Lam. In their place are two blue velvet sofas framed in garish gold leaf. Tony has always had a taste for opulence, but these new pieces are over the top—even for him. And the Roman column planters flanking the indoor-outdoor temperature-responsive crystalline paneling? Not just ostentatious—downright ugly. At least the panels live up to their name; though it's freezing outside, the glass keeps the interior perfectly toasty. I forget how effective the temperature-controlling glass is when I'm outside in the hedges, shivering in the cold.

A heavy marble-and-gold coffee table, another recent addition, anchors the room with its gaudy extravagance. A snarl rises in my chest. *It's her. It's all her.*

Even with these garish design changes, the house still feels like mine as I climb the floating stairs to the second floor. Each step floods me with memories, reminding me of the life I once had here. I'd forgotten how grand it felt to wake up in this place, to believe I'd finally arrived—surpassing every expectation I ever dared to imagine for myself. I wouldn't end up like my mother, cycling through painful relationships with men who only brought trouble. She never owned anything valuable. Never had stability.

I shake those thoughts away—I can't go there.

"I am his wife," I whisper into the stillness, letting each word settle around me like armor. *I. Am. His. Wife.*

But my resolve falters when I reach our bedroom doorway and see the rumpled sheets. *They were here—together—before jetting off on vacation.* My eyes close tightly, the image pressing against the inside of my eyelids like a bruise. Am I a fool? The question hangs heavy, unspoken, and I shake my head, refusing to admit what I'm not ready to accept.

It's fine. No one knows what I'm feeling—no one sees the cracks in my resolve. It's my secret, so I can keep hoping, even as the walls close in on me.

I inhale deeply, willing the nausea to subside, but it clings, unrelenting. Forcing my focus, I move with precision through Tony's walk-in closet—almost half the size of his bedroom. Everything is as meticulously arranged as I remember: cufflinks lined in a glass case, shirts hung by style, color, and fabric, shoes displayed neatly on their racks. I sift through his drawers carefully, not disturbing even a sock. Tony would notice.

And then, I find one item. Then another. Then three, four, five... *her things. Her drawers.*

Be still, I tell myself. *Close your eyes. Control your breathing. Focus on something else—anything that feels better.* This means nothing. She's his mistress. She barely leaves this house anymore. So what if he gave her drawers? He said he was losing interest in her, didn't he? He told me he still loved me, didn't he?

My thoughts reel. That was such a big day—our wedding day. We were a real couple. *How could it all end like this?* The thought feels too surreal.

I open my eyes, grounding myself, my feet planted firmly on the floors I thought I'd walk on forever. Determined now, I storm off, ready to find the answers I came here for.

And I know exactly where to look.

CHAPTER TWENTY-TWO

The silence of Tony's office presses on me, heavy and unsettling. Nothing stirs—not even a hint of dust drifting through the air. The room feels too still, as though it's holding its breath, waiting. The blinds are drawn shut, and the muted light filtering in from the hallway barely softens the oppressive darkness. I linger in the doorway, absorbing the familiarity, the essence of Tony that clings to every corner of this space. It's almost too much.

Then my gaze falls on the computer, sleek and unobtrusive, yet brimming with the answers I need. A magnetic pull draws me forward. Without hesitation, I move to the desk and slide into his chair.

As I sit, a dizzying rush of emotions crashes over me. This chair, this desk—this is his command center, his domain. I shouldn't be here. But that doesn't stop me. I power on the computer, and instantly, a password box blinks to life, expectant and unyielding.

I know his phone passcode. He'd once asked me to unlock it while he drove, trusting me to read and draft a quick message. At the time, I thought that moment was proof of something real—of trust, of faithfulness. But now, staring at this locked screen, I wonder if I ever truly knew him at all.

I type in his phone passcode—error.

"Damn it," I mutter, my fingers drumming against the desktop.

Tony isn't one for complex passwords. Despite his programming expertise, he prefers simple, meaningful combinations. My own passwords are labyrinthine strings of numbers and letters, drilled into me by my legal training—but Tony? His phone passcode is just his mother's birthday plus twenty-six—his "golden age," as he likes to call it.

I try her birthday, his younger brother Reign's, even variations on his own birthdate. Each attempt is met with rejection, the same cold error message flashing back at me every time.

The answer hovers on the tip of my tongue, bubbling just beneath the surface of my mind. I just need to think harder, push further.

I lean back in Tony's chair, which creaks softly under my weight, and let out a long, weary breath. I could give up, rifle through his desk drawers for clues, but deep down, I know the truth isn't there. Tony's too careful for that. The answers are here, locked inside this machine, guarded by a code that I know I can break.

Think, Sienna. Think. Who else means a lot to Tony?

Tony carries a deep-seated resentment for his father —a man who divorced his mother, Vonita, when Tony was just eight. Everything he knows about his father has been shaped by Vonita's bitter narratives. She's never spoken about him with kindness or warmth. To be honest, I can't even remember his father's name. But one detail has always stood out: February 8th.

That day, Tony couldn't get out of bed. He skipped work and barely ate. When I asked if he was feeling sick and offered to cancel my classes to stay home and take care of him, he pulled me close and said softly, "No need for all that. Today is my father's birthday."

I remember murmuring a sympathetic "Oh," and that was enough to open the floodgates. Tony spoke of his parents' fraught relationship, of the bitterness that lingered even after his father's death. I knew he had died of pancreatic cancer, but the sly, cutting remarks Tony usually made about him never hinted that his birthday would be a day of mourning.

Still, I remember the date: February 8th. Tony once told me his father died at thirty-six in 2078, when Tony was twelve. Piecing the numbers together, the fragments align until a possible password forms in my mind—clear as day.

I type it in, my fingers steady but my heart pounding, half-expecting the screen to reject it.

But it doesn't.

The password works. I'm in.

I sit up straight. My conscience whispers that I should stop, that going further is wrong. But what am I supposed to do? He's still my husband, yet he's out there gallivanting with her, planning to propose while he's still legally married to me. And I? I've been playing it too nice, letting him treat me like an afterthought.

No. No more.

I won't stop.

CHAPTER TWENTY-THREE

My eyes land on the Messenger icon. Forty-nine unread messages. My heart lurches as I open it, expecting mine to be among those ignored. But as I scroll, I see every message I've sent him—every desperate plea, every *I miss you,* every *I still love you.*

All marked as read.

He saw them. Every single one. And he chose to ignore me.

The discovery leaves me numb, like a sadness hovering just out of reach, lingering on the edge of realization. There's still more to uncover, more answers waiting, and I'll hold the pain off just a bit longer. I have to keep going.

I stare at the screen, feeling as though every word, every line I read pulls the air straight out of my lungs. The first message from him: *I love you, Bae.*

And her reply: *Back at you to the moon and back.*

I feel hollow, gutted. A dizzy sensation sweeps over

me, threatening to tip me off balance, but I cling to the chair and keep scrolling.

Part of me wants to stop. I wish I could. I wish that message was the only one. But there's so much more.

The messages continue—details of stolen moments, lunchtime rendezvous, calls to leave work early to spend the afternoon tangled together. They talk about their nights out, like dinners with Sara and her match, Alexander.

Tanya tells Tony to be polite, and he asks, Why do you care so much about Alexander's feelings? Do you want him?

Her reply is coy, brushing it off with humor. But it's the tone—flippant, possessive, careless with him, careless with *my husband*—that claws at me.

It feels like watching a life I was meant to live slip further and further away.

> Tanya: Saturday, October 24, 2099, at 9:33 AM
>
> He knows a lot of people, Tony. Just stop being an asshole when it comes to him. Love you.

I can't stop scrolling through their messages, unraveling the story of their lives together. It's too much to bear, yet I can't stop consuming it—their life, the one I always wondered about. Their relationship feels so ordinary, so real—not distant or abstract, but painfully tangible.

He jokes with her about never cooking; they eat out nearly every night. Occasionally, Tony cooks pasta—a quick, lazy dish for their evenings together. I used to cook for him almost every day, elaborate meals: slow-baked brisket, honey-encrusted salmon, and his favorite, my orange chicken. The fact that I cook and she doesn't feels like a small victory, a score for me. For a fleeting moment, I almost smile.

Then I stumble upon their early emails, and something in them feels off. My brows knit as I check the date on a message where she says she can't stop thinking about him, that it's driving her crazy.

I double-check the date. Then triple-check.

It's from *before* we even started wearing the YPM bands.

I blink, struggling to make sense of it, my throat tightening as a faint sting burns my eyes. But I can't stop now. Deception builds with every block of text, each one twisting the knife deeper.

And then I find it—a single message that stops me cold.

> Monday, April 13 at 9:03 AM
>
> I enjoyed every bit of being with you in Catalina. I miss your body already. I need you tonight.

> Tanya: Monday, April 13, 2099 at 9:04 AM
>
> Come over. Now.

He responded with a thumbs up.

Do you see this asshole? He was supposed to be at work by nine o'clock in the morning, but instead, he's leaving to go fuck her. And Catalina? *That's our place.*

I squeeze my eyes shut, concentrating, digging through my memories. The days in April, the week I spent alone… Wait. I remember now. That was the week before Monday, April 13th. I missed him so much I ached. Tony had told me he was heading to a digital ethics conference in Chicago.

So, not only did he lie about going to a conference, but on that Monday, he came home exhausted—*too tired to talk, too tired to touch me.* And yet, he still managed to journey off to work the next morning, only to leave his desk for a quickie with Tanya?

I close my eyes so tightly it feels like thunder erupts in my ears. *No.* I don't want to believe what this all reveals. Those messages—the love, the shared memories —leading up to the very day he handed me my YPM band with feigned excitement, pretending it was his first time too, as if we were embarking on a new journey together.

It was all an act.

The realization hits me like a dam breaking, and I spring out of the chair. Anger and hurt, so carefully contained for so long, surge forward with a fury I can't hold back. My mouth opens, releasing a scream that cracks through the air—a raw, primal sound that tears out of me and echoes through the silence.

I storm through the hallways, heading toward our bedroom, my vision blurred by hot, stinging tears. The need to destroy, to unleash, courses through me. I want to punch something, break something, rip apart every-thing I can lay my hands on. This house, this life, *this man*—they were all supposed to be mine.

"No," I growl, my voice trembling, each step harder than the last. "No!" The word tears from me like a battle cry, my heart pounding in defiance even as my face streams with tears.

"This is my house! My life too!" I scream, my voice bouncing off the walls, slicing through the silence like a jagged knife. My temples throb from the sheer force of it, but I don't care. Let it hurt.

I reach our bedroom and strip off my clothes with frantic urgency, as if shedding the weight of everything I've been holding inside. I climb into the bed that once felt like my sanctuary, the place where I believed love could keep us safe.

The luxurious sheets wrap around me as I pull them tight, burying myself in the remnants of what once was. Tears spill hot and unchecked down my cheeks, and I choke out a promise into the emptiness:

"I will not let him take this life away from me."

TUESDAY, NOVEMBER 17, 2099

CHAPTER TWENTY-FOUR

"Mrs. Holloway?"

A chipper, overly curious voice jolts me from sleep, its familiarity both jarring and unsettling. It stirs something deep within me—a longing for the days when that same voice used to ask, "Mrs. Holloway, what tasks would you like me to focus on today?" Or, "Would you like new scents in the bathrooms? I have Meyer lemon, orange blossom, and black licorice with lime." She always knew Tony's favorites. Back then, my only challenge was to choose the right one.

"Black licorice with lime," I recall saying once.

That evening, Tony came home late from work. He caught the scent lingering in his office bathroom and told me he loved it, said it would help him focus and keep him working until he was ready to come to bed. But he never came to bed—not even in the early hours of the morning. By the time I woke up, he was already gone, quietly slipping back to the office.

I have no idea why that memory surfaces now. Perhaps it's because everything about this moment feels wrong. I'm not supposed to be here, and I know it. The weight of that realization presses down on me, dragging me back into the agony I thought I'd cried away before falling asleep.

Tears well in my eyes as I look up. Standing there is Nessa, Tony's twice-a-week maid. Her expression is a mix of confusion and forced cheerfulness. She's here, and I—well, I'm not supposed to be.

I quickly untangle myself from the bedcovers and rise to my feet. "Nessa, oh my God."

"Are you okay?" she asks, her tone tentative. "Are you back?"

There's hope in her eyes, the kind of hope that pierces straight through me. Nessa's always liked me more than Tony—an oddity, considering everyone loves Tony. But she sees something in him, something unkind, something I couldn't—or wouldn't—acknowledge back then.

"No. I just…" My voice falters as I realize how disheveled and exposed I must look—hair tangled, clothes wrinkled, my face a canvas of sleepless despair. The air feels heavy, pressing down on me, thick with something I can't quite place—judgment, pity, or maybe both.

But Nessa doesn't step away to call the police, branding me unstable. Instead, her gaze softens, and what I see in her eyes catches me off guard—pure, unfiltered sympathy.

"Would you like me to make you tea or coffee?" she offers kindly, her voice gentle.

Even as I shake my head, every fiber of my being screams for escape. I can't risk Tony finding out I'm here.

But the truth is, I slept well in my former bed—better than I have in months. No tossing, no bad dreams, just a blank slate of peaceful nothingness. My body feels refreshed, no aches, no stiffness. The only pain is in my heart, a pain so raw and deep it feels unbearable.

"What day is it?" I ask, my voice unsteady, barely above a whisper.

"It's Tuesday," Nessa replies, her tone tentative, as though she's afraid her answer might shatter me.

"The 17th?"

"Yes."

I sigh, a small exhale of genuine relief. Part of me had expected to learn I'd slept for days, lost in the oblivion of exhaustion and despair. But now comes the hard part.

"Nessa," I begin, my voice faltering, laced with pleading.

"Yes, Mrs. Holloway?"

"Could you... not mention that I was here? I..." My voice wavers, and I close my eyes, searching for the right words. How do I explain that I'm unraveling, caught in the storm of Tony's betrayal and my own desperation?

"No," she says quickly, firmly. "I won't say a thing." Her gaze meets mine, full of warmth and unspoken understanding.

A shaky sigh escapes me, deeper this time, a rush of relief I hadn't realized I needed. "Thank you," I murmur, my voice barely holding steady.

"You're welcome. And… you don't have to leave right away," she offers gently, her kindness wrapping around me like a soft blanket.

Her words feel like a balm, a flicker of light piercing through the suffocating darkness. But I know I can't linger here. This isn't my life anymore. I need to go back to my apartment, gather my strength, and figure out what comes next. It's time to stop playing Tony's game on his terms. But how? Where do I even begin?

"My coat?" I ask, spinning in place as the realization hits—I don't have it.

"I hung it up downstairs, next to the front door," Nessa replies, her tone calm and reassuring.

I nod, murmuring my thanks. "What time is it?"

"Seventeen minutes after eight," she says, glancing at the clock before turning her attention back to me.

I gasp. My first class of the day starts at nine. Shit. My life is spinning out of control. Thanking Nessa one last time, I rush out the front door, knowing there's no time to go home and make myself presentable.

Once I'm on the Swift, I pull out my phone and check Tony's security footage. Relief washes over me when I see there's no recording of me—just a log showing I disarmed the system. Quickly, I delete the notification. Tony never checks the logs; he only notices if the alarm isn't set when he gets home. Nessa will rearm it when she leaves.

For now, I'm safe—safe from being caught, at least.

But not from the reality of what I've done. I broke into his house, violated his privacy, and committed an illegal act to uncover Tony's lies. The weight of it presses down on me like a vise. What do I do next? I can't just let this go. Something must be done. But what? I have no idea.

CHAPTER TWENTY-FIVE

I've been extra careful since Lena's scolding. My mind hasn't been too preoccupied with preparing for this class to stop thinking about Tony, though. He refuses to leave my thoughts, and the constant presence of him in my mind leaves me on edge.

I'm not an outright liar. That's one lesson my mother drilled into me: never lie. And yet, not lying hasn't exactly made me honest. Maybe that's why I've become so sneaky, skulking around Tony's house, even breaking in. Although, technically, I still have access.

But here I am, spinning webs of lies in my head, trying to figure out how to confront Tony about deceiving me—about lying about when he first wore his YPM band and the true timeline of his relationship with Tanya. Do I say Ethan's ticket turned up some interesting results and hit him with the evidence—bam? The thought alone makes me cringe. Part of me wishes I could just pretend I never saw those messages, never discovered what I now know.

Even now, as students file into my class and I force a vague smile at each one, I wish I'd never snooped.

The seats are half-filled. Only the overachievers—the ones fanatical about their grades—are here on time. They watch me intently, their eyes fixed on my mouth, waiting for me to feed them whatever it takes to get an A. The rest look bored, slouched in their chairs, their energy already drained. Once upon a time, the bored ones were my measure of success. If I could ignite a spark in their disinterest, I knew I was doing something right.

But now, as I scan the room, my gaze lingers on the eager students—their metaphorical baby bird mouths wide open, ready to be fed. And I wonder: Have I been nurturing the wrong flock? Have I ignored the loyal, faithful ones to indulge my own selfish impulses, my Id? The thought gnaws at me, sharp and unrelenting, but before I can unravel it further, the clock strikes 9:00.

It's time to begin.

CHAPTER TWENTY-SIX

Well, that went... interestingly. I tried my hardest to concentrate, to deliver something worthwhile, but I probably came across like an AI robot—mechanical, devoid of any spark. Two more classes remain on the docket today, and while I'd love to cancel them, I can't. At least I canceled office hours. No excuses, no explanations—just a curt message sent to all my students: *Office hours are canceled this week.* No one responded. Maybe they didn't care, or worse, maybe they've already written me off.

I could feel it during my lecture earlier—the silent judgment, the unspoken consensus that I'm no longer useful to them. That whatever spark once made me their favorite lecturer is gone.

But, oddly enough, Tony isn't on my mind right now. Instead, my thoughts drift to my mother. It feels strange. The tightness in my chest grows as I stare at my phone, contemplating. If I call her, will she answer? Why do I feel like she won't? She's my mother. Isn't she supposed to drop everything when I call?

Vonita drops everything for Tony. She never lets his calls go beyond a few rings. He doesn't even bother with pleasantries. He starts with, "Mom…" and dives straight into his grievances, seeking her validation. And she gives it—every single time. No matter how trivial, she reassures him, reinforces his stance.

I used to roll my eyes at her blind loyalty, maybe because I resented it. But now, I wonder… what would my life have been like if I hadn't had to work so hard just to keep her attention on me?

My phone is in my hand now, my skin flushed as I scroll through my contacts. My mom's name, Rush, stares back at me.

After I left Rush's chaotic world for college, I stopped calling her "Mom." For years, whenever I had to mention her, I would simply say "she," as if even acknowledging her was too much.

When I turned twenty-one—fully legal and no longer afraid she'd find a way to steal my independence —I started calling her Rush.

My heart braces itself as her phone rings. Rush has always inspired nothing but anxiety in me.

Once. Twice. Three times. Four.

After the fifth ring, disappointment settles in as her automated voicemail cuts through the silence: "Leave a message for Rush Pryor after the beep."

I pause, hesitating, the name pulling me into memories I'd rather avoid. Rush Pryor. She married some guy three years ago. Her last name changes every time she marries a new man.

"Hey..." My voice falters. I feel a pang of something —vulnerability? Weakness? A deep sadness? Regardless, I push forward. "Rush. So, um... I never told you this, but Tony and I have separated. Well, actually, he left me. You see, he cheated. In more ways than one." I pause, giving the tightness in my throat a chance to ease. "That sounds familiar, doesn't it? A cheating man."

I squeeze my eyes shut, frustration bubbling up inside me. I didn't mean to be so hostile.

Actually, Rush likes me better when I'm my best self. She pays more attention to me when I'm positive and achieving. She loves taking credit for my success, my happiness—not my failures or my miseries. So I quickly recalibrate.

"Sorry. I didn't mean to say that. But he deceived me in all kinds of ways, and yet... I still love him. It's like I'm possessed by this love for someone who's arguably..." I stop myself, pressing my lips together. I don't want to say it. Not yet. "But what is that, Rush? Do you know? Can you help me understand why I feel this way?"

The beep cuts me off, its suddenness almost a relief.

"If you would like to re-record, press one. If you would like to delete, press two. If you would like to send, press pound."

My hand trembles over the phone, my chest tight from the vulnerability I've just spilled out. Feeling faint and breathless, I press two.

Delete.

I sit with myself for a while, the silence pressing against me. The walls of my small office feel like they're closing in, and yet, I don't want to escape. I want to embrace it—the crushing weight, the confinement. I want to be obliterated. Gone.

This is not good.

CHAPTER TWENTY-SEVEN

I performed much better during my final two classes of the day. I pretended I was an actress, playing the role of a woman whose life resembled what I'd once imagined mine would be. Her Tony had a valid reason for not being forthright—perhaps he knew the truth would upset her, but he couldn't resist trying the YPM band. He hadn't believed it would actually work. *Think about it, Sienna,* I told myself. *He had no idea who Tanya was until their first meeting. That meant it wasn't Tanya's flawless beauty that drew him in; it was the manipulation of the technology.*

All the evidence points to YPM technology actually working—even though it hadn't worked for me.

Regardless, the fantasy carried me through.

But by the time my final class of the day ended, and I could finally shed the character I'd been playing, reality weighed heavier than ever. I realized it was time to face something I'd been avoiding for too long: reading meticulously through our divorce agreement.

I've been a bad lawyer. A terrible one, really. I hadn't even read the papers properly. Stupid, I know. I'd let Hansel, the lawyer Tony is paying to represent me "on my behalf," skim the critical parts for me, trusting Tony wholeheartedly. But now? Now I have enough doubt to question whether he's done me dirty in our agreement or if he's actually been fair.

As soon as I reach my apartment, ready to strip off my work clothes and slip into something comfortable, I notice a paper taped to my door. I think I'm the only tenant who still receives paper notices—probably because the lease is in Tony's name. All electronic notices are sent to him, not me. This apartment was supposed to be his way of taking care of me through all the YPM nonsense. I never doubted he had my best interests at heart. Why would I? He's such a good actor.

He seemed so torn up about our breakup—so embarrassed, so tortured by his lack of control over his feelings.

I shake the thought away before it can spiral into despair and unlock the door with my thumbprint. My stomach sinks as I glance at the notice in my hand: a warning. Only half the rent was paid last month, and now late fees have been tacked on. If the remainder isn't paid within five days, I'll face eviction.

I groan. Great. Another worry pressing down on me. I'll send Tony a text about the rent. I know he won't answer, but will he pay? I have enough savings to cover it—but already? He's stopped paying the rent already?

Shaking my head, I grab my phone and fire off a message to Tony, keeping it brief and to the point. I don't expect a reply, but at least I've done my part. Then, I strip off my work clothes, trading them for soft lounge pajamas that offer some comfort.

I pour myself a glass of red wine—my small indulgence to take the edge off—and settle onto the sofa. The warm glow of my floor lamp fills the room as I spread the divorce papers across the coffee table. It's time to confront the fine print. Time to find out if Tony's betrayal runs deeper than I thought.

CHAPTER TWENTY-EIGHT

To extend our divorce, Tony would revise his proposals. As I read through each draft, a disturbing trend emerged—he's offering me less and less with every revision. For instance, the first draft agreement included five thousand dollars a month for two years and half the rent for as long as I stayed in this apartment. His justification was always the same: to help me get on my feet. That's his mantra. "I want to continue to help you get on your feet."

The thing is, I never thought I was off my feet until he convinced me I was.

Then came the second draft, which I blindly signed. He dropped the monthly payment by a thousand dollars. And now, as I pore over the latest agreement—the one Hansel sent me last Friday but I hadn't read thoroughly until now—I see the rent provision is completely gone. On Friday, Hansel had read me the highlights of the agreement, conveniently leaving out the part where Tony decided to stop covering the rent entirely.

I take off my reading glasses and rub my exhausted eyes. The skin beneath them feels swollen, a protest against everything I've just consumed. I feel like I'm trapped in an alternate reality where none of my life makes sense. We were once happily married, totally in love—and now this? No one ever imagines this happening so early in a marriage. Absolutely no one.

What about our marriage ceremony, goddamn it! I think, frustration bubbling over. Tony cried that day—he kissed me before Dot, his friend who officiated the ceremony, even finished saying he could kiss me, his bride. That was love. That was desire. I'm not crazy. Tony showed me love. But now? Now, he's showing me nothing but disdain.

Could Quantum Matching's YPM band really make him despise me?

My phone buzzes, snapping me out of my spiraling thoughts. A new message. My stomach flips with hope. Is it him? Has he finally answered my text about the rent?

Tony My Love: 6:46 PM

Sorry about the rent. I'll talk to Demetria in the office. Don't worry.

Relief washes over me, filling me with a lightness I haven't felt in days. Yet beneath that relief, questions churn, bubbling up, impossible to ignore.

> 6:47 PM
>
> Have you asked Tanya to marry you?

No beating around the bush. A direct question calls for a direct answer. I stare at the screen, my breath catching each time the ellipses appear, vanish, and reappear. Each second feels like an eternity until his response finally arrives.

> Tony My Love: 6:54 PM
>
> Sorry for the delay. Miss you. Took a short trip to clear my head.

I GRIMACE, READING THE MESSAGE OVER AND OVER. He ignored my question. And what a way to minimize his romantic escapade with Tanya, calling it a "short trip to clear my head." He's definitely playing me. I want to fume, to scream—but I can't. I'm too used to this by now.

Before I uncovered the truth, I might've let him get away with dodging questions he didn't want to answer. But not anymore. My insides twist into knots as I force myself to push further.

> 6:56 PM
>
> You didn't answer my question. Did you propose to Tanya? Yes or No?

This time, his response is fast.

Tony My Love: 6:56 PM

No. I have to go. Good night. We'll talk
when I get home.

I sit very still, my mind spinning while my body feels
frozen. What now?

I shouldn't feel settled—not this strange, misplaced
calm. Not this fleeting confidence that Tony will
somehow take care of me again. I shouldn't feel, even
with him off gallivanting with Tanya, that I'm still in the
running to win his love back.

Our wedding day. Our first kiss. Our lovemaking.
The thousands of times he swore he loved me. None of
that should matter now. Not when I have an important
decision to make—a life-altering one.

I must force myself to think like a lawyer, not like a
fool.

MONDAY, NOVEMBER 23, 2099

CHAPTER TWENTY-NINE

TONY

My head feels like a locomotive is ripping through it. That "mini-break," as Tanya called it, was a wild ride—too long, way too expensive, and completely unnecessary. Subconsciously, I think I was trying to keep up with Alexander Creston, who wasn't even there. That guy just gets to me.

I'm losing my mind. Hell, I barely recognize myself anymore. Sure, I've always appreciated the finer things, but blowing nearly half a million dollars on a five-day luxury superyacht cruise? That's insane. The trip was a whirlwind of five-star dining, cliff-diving, scuba diving, jet-ski adventures, private island beach days—so much, too damn much to do.

There were eight of us: Tanya and her friends—Jonae, Blue, and Blue's husband Dan. Then my group—Rebecca, Jim, and Jim's quantum match, Lilith. Every single one of them could've chipped in for the final tip or at least covered their portion of the private flights to and from Sydney. Even Tanya. But nope. I footed the bill for everything.

Now, I'm staring at my bank accounts, usually stacked and comfortably so. The numbers say I only have fifteen thousand and some change in disposable cash. What the fuck. And on top of that, Sienna wants me to pay her rent.

"Jeez," I mutter, rubbing my eyes to ease the tension building behind them. Women are expensive. Tanya is expensive. And I can't stop wanting to make her happy. She's going to drain me dry, even before…

My shoulders slump under the weight of an unspoken truth, and I instinctively rub the back of my neck. Here's the truth: Tanya doesn't know it. Sienna doesn't know it either—only James and me. Tanya and I don't share a forever match.

That should be enough to make me think twice—hell, three times—before letting Tanya drain me dry. I should put a stop to this reckless spending. But I can't.

Then there's Alexander. I can't shake the feeling that, bond or not, she'd leave me for him if given the chance. Would he take her? I don't know, and maybe it doesn't even matter. What does matter is that I'll do whatever it takes to keep her with me.

Currently, I don't need to plan much beyond dealing with Sienna. I can't pay her rent—she'll have to figure that out on her own. My focus is on calling Demetria to see if I can get my name off the lease while leaving Sienna's on. I should've put her name on it from the start. What was I thinking? But I can handle this—

convince Demetria to make the changes. She's easy to persuade, like putty in my hands.

I close my eyes, pressing my fingers against them to ease the stinging pain shooting behind them. As I exhale, a sharp knock breaks through my thoughts. I glance up to see Sara standing outside the glass window, waving with a grin that's far too cheerful for my current mood. Suppressing a groan, I instinctively roll my shoulders back.

Sara gestures toward the doorknob, silently asking for permission to come in. My first instinct is to shake my head and point at my computer, signaling that I'm too busy. But curiosity tugs at me despite my irritation. There's something I've been meaning to ask her anyway.

Sara has a way of knowing what's going on. She's not a gossip, but she always stays in the loop. I've been trying to get ahold of James for days now. He's been dodging me, testing my patience with his disappearing act. His insubordination is becoming a problem. I need to remind him who's in charge, but I have to tread carefully. If anyone knows where James is hiding or what he's up to, it's Sara.

With a sigh, I wave her in. The door swings open harder than expected, the sharp motion making me flinch.

"Hey, Tony! You're back," Sara says brightly, her voice practically buzzing with excitement.

I lean back in my chair, keeping my annoyance in check with a polite nod. "Yeah, I'm back."

"How was it?"

I grunt and shrug. "It was okay."

"Oh." She drags the word out, like she's chewing on my answer, trying to puzzle it out. Then, without waiting for an invitation, she flops down on my couch, stretching her arm across the top as if settling in for a long conversation. "I ran into Sienna last week. She didn't look well."

Her gaze sharpens, her eyes boring into mine with a scrutiny that feels like it's trying to peel back layers. I work to keep my expression neutral, even as a pang of irritation rises. The last thing I need is Sara talking to Sienna. Sara has a way of planting seeds—ideas that could grow into something inconvenient, even dangerous.

"Yeah," I sigh, feigning sympathy. Not that I need to fake it entirely; I do feel for Sienna. A part of me hates what she's going through. But what am I supposed to do? Sacrifice my own happiness? Pretend I'm still in love with her when my heart is with someone else?

Sara tilts her head, studying me with unsettling curiosity. "She says she's not with her match. Something about a false match or something. Did you know that?"

Her words hang in the air, heavy with implication. I can feel her eyes on me, dissecting every flicker of emotion I can't quite suppress. My stomach knots. Did she come here just to grill me about Sienna?

"But," she continues, as though my discomfort doesn't register, "she met the guy, and he submitted a help ticket to look into things. That should help soon, but honestly, I'm worried about her."

My chest tightens. No shit, I've been worried too—

nonstop. But now, this? A help ticket? My throat goes dry, but I force myself to ask, "A ticket?"

"Yes," she says, her tone light, as if this is just idle gossip. "A help ticket. I'm surprised she hasn't told you. Have you spoken to her lately?"

Her words blur into a haze as my mind fixates on the implications. That ticket could unravel everything. I need to act fast—find James and shut this down before it spirals out of control. Sara's gaze, however, lingers on me, sharp and unrelenting. Is she fishing for something? Or worse—does she already know?

I shoot to my feet. "I have to go."

Sara stays seated, her expression calm but scrutinizing. Her look doesn't just make me uncomfortable—it cuts deep. It's like she sees through every carefully constructed wall I've built, every secret I've buried. But that's impossible. No one knows the full picture. Not even me some days.

As she rises slowly, her voice softens. "If you need to talk, Tony, unburden yourself maybe, I'm here."

A dry snort escapes me, loaded with sarcasm I don't bother to mask. Let her take it however she wants. Sara's one of those "stand by other women" types— always ready to swoop in, to feel sorry for someone like Sienna. That's fine. But she needs to stay the hell out of my business.

CHAPTER THIRTY

TONY

Finally, Sara's out of my office, but the tension she left behind clings to the air, suffocating. No way am I going to bring up James with her—not when she might already be sniffing around too much. For now, as far as Sara's concerned, I'll lay low.

On my way to track James down, I call him. The phone doesn't even ring—it goes straight to voicemail. *Blocked.* My jaw tightens, and my pace quickens, footsteps heavy as I approach his office. Just before reaching the door, I force myself to slow. Storming in guns blazing isn't going to work. James doesn't respond well to threats. He needs reassurance, not aggression. All I need is for him to make a few more tweaks on the YPM mainframe, and then we're done. I'll even sweeten the deal if that's what it takes. He's already well-paid as a top-tier programmer, but I can make it worth his while.

I push the door open, only to find his desk empty.

What's her name again?

The woman seated at the adjacent desk greets me

with a grin, completely oblivious to the storm brewing inside me. "Hi," she says, her tone cheerful. I forgot to wear my "cool, calm, and collected" mask. I put it on now.

Then I remember. "Lisbon, hello."

Her cheeks flush slightly as she tucks a curl behind her ear. "Um, hi," she repeats, her voice softer.

"Have you seen James?" I ask, cutting to the chase.

"James doesn't work here anymore," she says, nodding toward his empty desk as if to hammer the point home.

The desk is spotless—no computer, no clutter, not even a speck of dust. James always kept things tidy, but not like this.

"Where did he go?" My voice falters, a note of panic slipping through.

Lisbon shrugs. "I don't know. He didn't say." She raises her eyebrows, a hint of amusement playing on her face. "That's the mystery."

"Shit," I mutter, the word escaping in a low growl. My mind reels. What the hell does he think he's doing? Fighting back? Running? Playing me?

I leave the room, walking the halls aimlessly, my thoughts a cacophony of anger and regret. What have I done? Did I really need to push him so hard? Was it all worth it—everything I've done to cover my tracks?

A passing colleague nods at me, offering a polite greeting. I return it with a tight smile, but the realization hits me like a punch to the gut: people are watching. My perfectly curated image—the confident, in-control professional—is unraveling before their eyes. I need to pull it together, fast. They're used to seeing me as the one who always has it together, who commands respect. Not this.

Not the guy at risk of losing his job, his career, and what little self-respect he has left.

And if I go broke, I'll lose Tanya.

That, above all else, cannot happen.

CHAPTER THIRTY-ONE

Purging my mind of unnecessary thoughts, I find myself back in my office. With a long, measured exhale, I take my seat at the desk. First things first: Sienna. She needs to be out of my orbit —sooner rather than later.

I call Hansel, my finger tapping impatiently on the desktop. The last thing I need is another person I'm paying handsomely dodging me when I need them.

Finally, the line connects.

"Tony?" Hansel sings, cheerful as ever. His tone aggravates me. How does this guy sound like he doesn't have a care in the world when I'm paying him to help clean up my messes? Shouldn't he at least act like he feels some of my burden?

"Hey, Hansel," I snap, cutting through his unwarranted cheeriness. There's no time for small talk—this is business. "I need you to pull the last agreement you sent to Sienna and finalize the previous one."

"Oh…"

The hesitation in his voice makes my jaw clench. "What?" I demand.

"Well…" His tone shifts, cautious. "Two things. First, Sienna let me go."

A cold knot forms in my stomach. "She *what*?"

"And second…" He hesitates again, and I can feel my patience hanging by a thread. "She filed a response to the agreement."

The words hit me like a punch to the gut. For a moment, all I can hear is the rushing in my ears. What the hell has she done now?

CHAPTER THIRTY-TWO

The students file into my second class of the day, their chatter a low hum that barely registers. I've been crying—a lot—and it shows. My eyes are puffy, red, and swollen, and my face reflects every ounce of the turmoil I'm feeling. But I can't summon the energy to care anymore. I look the way I look because my life is spiraling out of control.

Still, I'm here. Ready to teach. Or at least, trying to appear ready.

I hate that I had to respond to Tony's latest agreement the way I did. His terms were harsh, almost cruel —so unloving they seemed like a deliberate slap in the face. They completely contradict the way he kept insisting he still loved me. His version of love is starting to feel more like punishment than affection.

As I glance around the classroom, every face stares back at me with the same expression: curious, cautious, quietly judgmental. They're trying to piece me together, and honestly, I don't blame them. If I were in their shoes, I'd wonder about the mental stability of the person who holds the power to grade me at the end of the quarter.

Not that grades matter much anymore. Most of them will receive high marks anyway. That's just where I'm at now—too worn down to care about something as trivial as grades.

respond. I asked him to continue paying my rent—after all, he was the one who insisted I leave our home and move into that expensive apartment. I also requested thirteen thousand a month in spousal support —the full amount I'm legally entitled to once all the accounting is done. Writing that was agonizing. Advocating for myself felt unnatural, almost wrong. I kept wanting to soften the terms, to make the request less... demanding. I was so close to caving, but I stuck to my guns.

I close my eyes, shaking my head as frustration churns in my chest. Who am I? What have I become?

A vibration from my phone on the lectern in front of me snaps my attention back to the present. Class is about to start, but I glance down anyway, my breath catching when I see the name on the screen.

It's Tony. My heart stops for a beat.

> Tony My Love: 10:57 AM
>
> I have something to confess. I lied. I was with Tanya before I gave you a YPM band.

Choked by shock, I struggle to breathe. Why is he telling me this now? Is he testing me? Did he somehow find out I entered the house and went through his computer? Is he trying to lure me into confessing something he already knows I did?

Immediately, another message comes through.

> **Tony My Love: 10:58 AM**
>
> I'm sorry. I'm an asshole. Let's end this now. Spoke to Hansel. Sign the previous divorce settlement, please.
>
> Soon. Today. Then let's talk. I care for you still. I really do.

My confusion deepens with each passing second as I try to unravel the motivation behind this series of texts. Only now do I notice my hands trembling, my body shaking as if I've been hit by a sudden chill.

I look out over the sea of faces, my students waiting for me to speak.

"Professor Holloway, are you okay?" Juniper Singleton asks, her voice cutting through the haze like a distant echo.

"No," I chirp, the word escaping me before I can stop it.

What about our kiss at Neon Spice? What about *I love you*? Now I've been downgraded to *I care about you.* Is it because of my response to the agreement? That has to be it. That's why he's asking me to sign the previous settlement.

I could do it... if—

If…

I shut my eyes tightly, cutting off the rest of that thought because it feels impossibly heavy. Yet, a small spark of possibility flickers. Could that text have been Tony's way of getting my attention?

"I'm sorry," I say, my voice cracking. I clear my throat, trying again. "I'm sorry."

Every eye in the room is fixed on me.

How many times this quarter have I dismissed class early, fumbled through lectures, or just outright failed to be the professor they signed up for? I hate this version of myself—the one unraveling before them. But I must have this talk with Tony—not later, now.

"I have to dismiss you," I say, my voice trembling slightly. "An emergency came up."

A collective groan rises from the room, wrapping around my already frazzled nerves.

"I'm so sorry." I close my eyes briefly, trying to collect myself. I have to offer them something—an olive branch to ease the weight of their disappointment. "Today's lecture notes will be available for download this evening at seven p.m. I'll also upload three modules containing recent court decisions that will impact environmental law for at least the next three generations. On Wednesday, we'll discuss their implications in detail."

I exhale a long, relieved breath when I see their discontent begin to fade. They start to nod, some exchanging murmurs of interest. That was enough.

"Thank you," I say as most begin gathering their things. "I'll see you Wednesday."

Some stay behind, lingering for a moment, but I

gather my things and go. Tony needs to hear from me—face to face. If he's going to lie to me, he'll have to do it looking me in the eye. If he's going to profess his love, I want to feel it, see it in the flesh, and know if it's real.

Soon enough, I'll have my answers. I'm hoping for love. I *need* his love.

CHAPTER THIRTY-THREE

Thankfully, I drove to work today. Errands had me zigzagging across town before my first class. The traffic is still light, just as it was earlier when I stopped at MarketMax in the South Bay to stock up on much-needed toiletries. After that, I headed downtown to officially submit a notarized response to Tony's settlement proposal.

I'm not surprised Tony found out so quickly that I submitted my own terms. Hansel must have told him when he broke the news that I'd terminated his services —something else I handled this morning. They say only fools represent themselves in legal matters, but honestly, Hansel had done such a poor job advocating for me that my own efforts feel like a premium upgrade. If it comes to needing outside representation later, I'll deal with it then. For now, I feel safer without him.

As I drive, Tony's last text loops in my mind, and I can't stop dissecting its possible meanings. He didn't have to admit his affair with Tanya started much earlier than he led me to believe—but he did. Then he apologized. He even called himself an "asshole." Tony is rarely remorseful, so that has to mean something.

Yes, he said he wanted to "end things soon," but maybe that was shame talking. Tony doesn't need to shame himself. He's only human, and so am I.

Tony's always bolder over text. When he looks me in the eyes, I think he remembers more clearly how much he loves me. That's why he kissed me at Neon Spice. He needs me. I bet his head felt just as floaty as mine.

My first stop is Tony's workplace. I know where he parks his car. Before figuring out how to gain access to his work floor—it's security protected because of the nature of their work—I find a parking spot on the street. I pay six dollars for thirty minutes, which feels like highway robbery. I consider putting in more money just in case our conversation goes long. If I get a parking ticket, I'll happily pay it.

I'll remind Tony of our first kiss, the first time we made love, how we used to hold hands even while sleeping. I'll tell him how I made meals for him, how I turned his house into a home. I'm the more sensible choice.

And yes, I look pretty awful these days—stress has a grip on me that feels like it'll kill me if he doesn't choose me. But before the YPM band ruined our lives, I was beautiful, the kind of woman who turned heads wherever she went. I'm also nicer than Tanya. I'm kind and pleasant.

Tanya? She's... not. It's not like I've spent much time with her, but I've watched her. She wears entitlement and narcissism like a cheap suit that costs way too much money.

By the time I enter the parking garage, I've worked up a sweat—and a modicum of regret. I shouldn't be making such harsh judgments about Tanya. I'm just hurt. Still, she's with a married man. If I were her, I'd give Tony an ultimatum: divorce your wife first, and then I'll date you. Quantum energy match or not, no tug should be strong enough to thwart common decency.

It hits me that I shouldn't know where Tony parks his car. Another shameful secret bubbles to the surface— I've come to this garage many times over the past months just to confirm he's at work. There's something strangely comforting about knowing he's here, at the office, and not off with her.

But his car isn't in its assigned parking space. The spot is empty. He could be at home. Our home.

Without thinking, I sprint out of the parking garage, not stopping until I reach my car. Rain begins to patter against my windshield as I drive toward what used to be our home. Tony should consider himself lucky I wasn't the one to demand the house. Technically, I could've asked for it—I lived there longer than six months. I even sold my cute bungalow in Pasadena to start a life with him.

If I really wanted to, I could fight for what's mine and financially devastate him. But... I don't know.

Maybe I'm having these thoughts because I'm angry. Truly angry. The kind of anger I've never been good at expressing. I trap it inside, shoving it deep into a place where my Id takes over, twisting it into mean, dark imaginings.

It makes me think the worst of people, envisioning situations where they're reduced to nothing. And sometimes I wonder if that's worse than facing someone, screaming at them, hurling curses, and telling them to go to hell. At least that kind of rage is honest.

I exhale, pushing the anger out of my body. It won't do me any good when I finally see him. Besides, in truth, that's Tony's house. He worked very hard for it.

I still have some savings left from selling my bungalow, but it's not much. I had taken out so many loans on that house that, by the end, the profit wasn't as much as it should've been. And then, I think I started spending frivolously—no, let's call it what it was. I did spend frivolously.

I thought, finally, I was in a relationship where my money was mine, and his was ours. A designer purse here. A spa day there. Weekly salon appointments. And more. So much more.

I'll put it this way: if I don't have a job by mid-spring quarter 2100, I'll be pinching pennies again. The thought churns uneasily in my stomach. But it does something else, too—it emboldens me.

That's why, after parking on the street directly in front of the property and arriving at Tony's gate, I don't play coy.

I hold my breath as I press my thumb to the key lock plate. Since I started pushing back, there's a real chance this won't work. In a fit of anger, Tony might have done the sensible thing and locked me out of my old home.

But the gate whirs to life, rolling open without hesitation. Tony still hasn't scrubbed me from the security system, and for now, that's a small relief.

I ignore the way my shoulders want to curve inward with timidness, and the way fear claws at me, urging me to sink into the driveway's concrete. Instead, I keep my gait steady and posture upright as I walk toward the door. I force myself to project confidence—because I belong here. This house was ours, and I'm determined to remind Tony of that.

With each step, I cling to the hope that my wishes are on the verge of coming true. They will come true. This chapter of our lives is about to end, and a new one will begin. I can feel it.

CHAPTER THIRTY-FOUR

I use my fingerprint to unlock the main entrance to the house and step inside, forcing myself to stay bold and confident. There's no way I'm turning tail and running now.

"Tony?" I call, my voice steady as I gaze into the living room.

The sight before me is almost comical—Tanya's over-the-top and tacky taste makes me shake my head. I can't believe he let her do that to his living room. It's not just a change in décor—it's a takeover, one that feels as if it erases every trace of the life we once had here. My jaw tightens, but I force myself to stay composed. I didn't come here to critique Tanya's bad taste. I came for answers.

At the foot of the stairs, I call louder—"Tony!"

Someone's upstairs. I can feel it, hear it—the faint sound of footsteps. But the cadence is unrecognizable, and they're definitely not Tony's. For a second, the most horrific thought flashes through my mind. Is it someone else? Someone I shouldn't have to face?

I shake it off. It's probably Nessa, I tell myself. It's Monday, after all, and she often works on Mondays.

But then she appears, descending the stairs with an air of effortless grace. It's Tanya, draped in a long, red silk robe that clings perfectly to her figure, her face fully made up, as though she's seconds away from stepping into a photo shoot.

"What are you doing here?" she asks, her voice measured but tinged with something I can't quite place. Curiosity? Shock? Or maybe it's fear.

I'm here uninvited, looking eager and desperate. I must seem deranged to her. And maybe, just maybe, she's not entirely wrong.

I open my mouth to speak, but no words come out.

I hate to admit it, but she looks stunning—striking, even. Worse than that, she looks like she belongs here, like my home is her home.

My hands curl into fists at my sides as questions race through my mind. Now that I have her here, all to myself, there's so much I want to ask. But I can only manage one question, the one that feels like a sharp stone lodged in my chest.

"Why are you with my husband before we're even divorced?" The words spill out of me, shaky but resolute.

Tanya's head jerks back, her expression startled, almost offended. She glances over her shoulder, her eyes searching—maybe for help, maybe for an escape.

But then she pins me with an obstinate look. "That's

a you problem," she replies, her voice sharp and dismissive, like she's brushing off a stray thread from her silk robe.

I flinch. Her words hit me hard, disappointment crashing over me—sharp, suffocating. With that single reply, she's proven exactly who I thought she was—a selfish, heartless bitch.

"What about decency?" I shout. Although I fear my words have fallen on deaf ears.

She descends the stairs a bit more, still maintaining a safe distance, her posture confident but cautious. "You know, Sienna, I feel for you," she says, placing a hand over her chest like she actually has a heart. Her tone is syrupy, patronizing, as if I'm some sad little puppy she's pitying.

"Tony knows what he wants. That's why I'm here. He's leading you on for some"—she rolls her eyes—"odd reason."

She's mentioning my calls and my texts, but her words are merging into a blur, like a radio fading in and out, because all I can see is it.

The ring.

A large, stunning diamond that sparkles like it belongs on the cover of a magazine. It's sitting smugly on her finger, screaming at me louder than her words ever could.

"Sienna, go home. For once, have some self-respect," she says, her tone cutting.

"What?" I choke out, the word barely escaping my lips. The ring. I can't stop staring at it. My vision tunnels until that's all I can see. "Did he ask you to marry him?"

It's as if she just realized where my focus has landed. Her hand darts up, covering the ring with her other hand, like she's shielding it from me, like it needs protection.

"Tony and I share a bond," she says, her voice firm, tinged with superiority. "Why don't you finally meet your match so you can understand what this is we have? This can't be broken. He and I are in this forever. We have a forever match."

Her words pierce me like shards of glass, but I can't even find the strength to react. My mouth hangs open, useless, my tongue thick and swollen. There's so much I could explain to her, so much I should say. But why should I?

Reality crashes over me like hail the size of golf balls, each sharp impact leaving its mark. Every part of me aches, inside and out. It's over. It's all over.

"Gosh, you're so weak," Tanya says, rubbing in the fact that she's won. Her expression has twisted into pure disdain as she watches me.

But then her words hit me like a slap, igniting something raw and primal inside me. My hands clench into fists, my body burning with heat as fury courses through my veins. My breathing grows ragged, like an angry bull ready to charge.

I take a step toward her, my vision narrowing, my muscles taut with the possibility of action. I could jump on her. I could beat her to a pulp.

But the thought terrifies me.

The rage bubbling inside me becomes too much, and I step back, shaking, trying to regain control.

"What the hell?" Tony's voice cuts through the tension like a whip, sharp and commanding.

I whip my head around to see him standing in the doorway with worry etched into his features. He looks haggard, almost unrecognizable—like someone who hasn't slept in days.

"What are you doing here, Sienna?" he demands, his tone a mix of exasperation and something close to worry—but not for me. For her.

Tears cloud my vision. This is too much heartache to bear, and the longer I stay here, the more it hurts. For the first time in a long time, I don't let myself linger on how good he smells, on how much I love the scent that once brought me so much comfort. I don't let myself imagine wrapping my arms around him, clinging to the man I once believed was mine. No. It's abundantly clear now—he is not mine.

And now, I'm empty.

I push past Tony, my long strides fueled by embarrassment, heartbreak, and a hopelessness so profound it feels like it's crushing my chest. Tears stream down my face, unstoppable, and I swipe at them furiously with the backs of my hands—left, right, left, right—sniffing as I go.

The gate is still open. He must've seen my car parked out front. That's why he looks the way he does—put off by me, worried about what I might've done.

He was afraid for her. Afraid for the woman he chose to protect. Not me. Never me.

The thought shatters me completely as I step through the gate and back into my empty, cold car. The second I close the door, the floodgates open. My sobs come hard and violent, shaking my entire body like an earthquake tearing through my core. I grip the steering wheel as though it's the only thing tethering me to this world.

I feel raw. Stripped bare. Exposed to the elements of every emotion I've been too afraid to face. And now they're all here—anger, betrayal, humiliation, despair.

Who do I have?

Where do I go from here?

I'm spiraling, my thoughts darker and heavier with each second. I need help, I realize. Because these thoughts—these crazy ideations—are pulling me under.

I don't want to exist anymore.

I can't exist, even if I tried.

The overwhelming sense of failure crushes me. How could I not have seen it? How did I let it get this far?

But then, through the cacophony of my breakdown, a voice rises. Quiet but clear, from a place deep within me.

One name.

CHAPTER THIRTY-FIVE

E than scheduled a 4:00 p.m. meeting with me in his home office. We couldn't meet at his workplace because the entire building is closed for net-zero renovations until after the new year. That was roughly two hours ago. The wait has felt like several lifetimes, but at least it's given me time to pull myself together—somewhat.

Now, I'm parked outside his home in Hancock Park, trying to steady my thoughts by focusing on the neighborhood.

Once, during law school, I visited an exhibit on historical Los Angeles. It struck me how much a handful of decades can transform a place. Old Hancock Park was described in reverent terms: stately mansions with red-tiled roofs, intricate wrought iron gates, and lush gardens nestled beneath the comforting shade of century-old trees. Those were the exhibit's exact words.

Standing in front of those photos of Tudor and Mediterranean Revival facades, I felt transported to an era when modernity stood at a crossroads—a time when people were torn between clinging to old beliefs, stoked by the powers that be, or embracing the limitless possibilities of the future. Looking around now, it's clear which vision won.

The neighborhood has transformed into a showcase of sleek, contemporary architecture. Streets are lined with homes featuring sharp edges, asymmetrical designs, and dramatic cantilevered living spaces. Dense hedges have given way to sculptural landscapes of native plants arranged in geometric patterns that mirror the clean lines of the homes. Solar panels, once conspicuous, are now seamlessly integrated into the architecture, powering these residences with an efficiency that renders old electrical grids nearly prehistoric.

And then there's the glass. So much glass. Temperature-responsive crystalline paneling regulates internal climates without a single thermostat. The material is virtually impenetrable and non-collapsible—a marvel of modern engineering. This neighborhood feels like a museum of the world's finest contemporary mansions.

I never pictured Ethan living in a place like this. I imagined him in a setting more like Lena's—classical, understated, quiet.

Boy... people can be so surprising, so different from what they seem.

I sigh, the sound trembling in the air. How do I even have the mental space to think about architecture right now? I'm so tired, so utterly worn out. Maybe it's the openness of this neighborhood, the newness of everything. Hancock Park didn't hold back when it embraced the future, and for some reason, that resonates with me right now.

I glance at the time on my car's screen. My wayward thoughts only took two minutes. It's time. Without delay, I grab my things and step out of the car. I have no idea what Ethan can offer me or what he might say to ease the crushing weight of grief pressing on me, suffocating me. But as I stand here, I realize what I want.

I want to be like Hancock Park. I want to move forward, to step into a better tomorrow.

Yet the path ahead feels foggy, hindered by a desperation I can't seem to escape.

I ring the doorbell, and Ethan answers quickly. We exchange our hellos—mine tight with a sudden rush of emotion at seeing him, the man who's volunteered to help me in my time of need, and his calm and inviting.

As he undoes the top two buttons of his crisp light blue shirt, his effortless smile and the natural twinkle in his eyes feel like a flush of warmth on an icy day.

"I apologize for rushing. I just got home," he says, leading me at a brisk pace down a hallway. We pass an atrium with a blooming cherry blossom tree that looks so vibrant it can't possibly be real.

"I didn't see you drive up," I remark, still stealing glances at the tree, trying to determine if it's artificial.

"There's a private residents' entrance road at the rear of the house," he explains.

"You have a nice home." I take in more of the elegant yet comfortable design of his space. "It's large for one person."

Ethan's twinkling eyes dim slightly, and a flicker of

sadness crosses them—just enough to suggest there's a story behind him living here alone. I wait, giving him a moment to share, but he doesn't.

Instead, he opens a rear door, leading me across a cement path through a perfectly manicured lawn to a quaint casita that holds its mid-century charm. It's obvious he doesn't intend to elaborate on why he lives in this big house alone. And why should he? I'm the one in crisis, not him.

CHAPTER THIRTY-SIX

I stand, taking in my surroundings as Ethan turns up the heat. The casita's atmosphere feels comfortable—tranquil, even. Pale wood floors stretch beneath big, inviting royal blue velvet furniture, including a sofa that practically begs me to sink into it and make myself at home.

"Please, have a seat," Ethan says, gesturing to the sofa with an understanding smile—the kind a doctor gives right before an exam.

And the sofa does its job. As soon as I sit, it all comes rushing back—my earlier confrontation with Tanya. Her expression flashes in my mind, the one she gave when I finally asked the question that had been haunting me for months: *Why are you with my husband before we're even divorced?*

Her answer hits me again like a slap to the face: *"That's a you problem."*

Since it happened, the memory has tried to haunt me, looping endlessly, her face—smug and unbothered

—playing over and over again in my head. I've fought hard to push those thoughts away, to keep them at bay. But now? Now, I'm allowing them in. I'm letting them haunt me. No holds barred.

Ethan settles into his armchair. "So," he says, his voice calm but direct, "what do you want me to do for you?"

I shake my head, pulling my coat tighter around me. It's still chilly in here. "I don't know. Maybe you can… make it all make sense."

"But it already makes sense, doesn't it? Because if you're searching for the 'sense,' then it does make sense."

I blink, thrown off by his circular logic. "What's that supposed to mean?"

He tilts his head slightly, studying me like I'm a puzzle he's working to solve. "I don't engage in shock therapy, Sienna. I'm not here to hand you answers on a silver platter. We all arrive at the same truths in our own time—through processing our lived experiences and emotions."

He picks up a notepad and pen from a nearby desk, his steady gaze never leaving me. "I recall you mentioned you're from Los Angeles."

My jaw tightens as I nod curtly, my body rigid. He's veering in a completely different direction than I expected. "Yes."

"How was it growing up? How was your childhood?"

I pin him with a sharp look, my discomfort bubbling to the surface. "What does that have to do with Tony?"

He nods thoughtfully, as if recalibrating, his pen tapping lightly against the pad. "Well… here's what I suspect. You tell me if I'm right or wrong."

My arms fold tighter across my chest. "Go ahead."

"I suspect your primary relationship was with your mother, and you rarely, if ever, voiced what you truly wanted to her. You followed her to hell and back, simply to protect her—and, in turn, yourself. Yet no matter how hard you tried, she could never make you feel safe or loved. And you tried very hard."

He cocks an eyebrow, his gaze steady and unrelenting. "How am I doing?"

My body stiffens, locked in place. His words hit like a bullseye, striking too close to something I've spent years avoiding—not even daring to admit it to myself.

And then, as if unbidden, one word rises to the surface of my mind. Tears well in my eyes as I finally speak it aloud. "Rush." My voice cracks. "That's her name. My mom. Rush." My lips press tightly together, the weight of the name nearly unbearable. I don't want to say more.

"When you think about Rush, what memory comes to mind?" Ethan asks, his voice soft, almost lulling. "Take your time."

My eyes widen, my brain resisting. I don't want to answer. "What does this have to do with what Tony and Tanya did to me earlier?"

"Well… how did they make you feel?" Ethan's tone remains steady, disarming.

My frown deepens, twisting my face. "Angry."

"What else?"

I close my eyes, scratching nervously at the back of my head, reluctant to go where I've never allowed myself to go. "Rejected."

"What else?"

"Embarrassed. Disrespected. Toyed with."

Ethan's voice doesn't waver. "How often does Rush make you feel those ways?"

My breath catches in my throat as the past surges forward, a tidal wave of memories crashing into me. A cascade of moments flashes through my mind, all pointing to the same truth.

I get it now. I understand.

The floodgates are about to open. And for the first time ever, another human being will learn who Rush really was to me.

CHAPTER THIRTY-SEVEN

Nearly an hour has passed, and I've poured everything out to Ethan—every detail about my mother and her three husbands. She never married my father, though he was the first.

I described how I watched her fall recklessly in love with each of them—hard, unloving men. Unkind. Uncaring. She gave everything to them, and they gave nothing in return. Except to me. To me, they gave a persistent, inescapable sense of unease, as if my very existence hinged on surviving them.

"But she wasn't all bad," I tell him, my voice faltering. "She would take me out for a treat when I brought home a report card with all As. No Bs. Only As." I pause, my chest tightening. "She loved telling people that her daughter is a straight-A student, as if that absolved her."

I squeeze my eyes shut tightly, trying to endure the icky feeling gripping me until it passes.

"I called her last week—on Tuesday," I add, my

voice barely above a whisper as tears well up again. "She never called me back. Maybe that's why. I didn't leave a message. Because I knew... I knew she didn't care to hear from me in the first place."

"That's normal," Ethan says, his tone calm and steady. "It's normal to want your parent to answer when you call. To expect it. My wife and I would always return our children's calls, even if they called by accident. It would send us into a tizzy, scrambling to find out if they were safe.

Because that's built into human nature, Sienna. It's part of our hardware. But if a parent isn't expressing that instinct, then something is broken."

He leans forward slightly, his expression sincere.

"I want you to understand that something was and still is broken in your mother. She used you and the outside world in an attempt to fix herself, but she can't be fixed unless she acquires the tools to fix herself from within.

And the same applies to you. Tony cannot fix you. I can give you tools, but you're the one who has to apply them. You're the one who has to fix yourself."

I nod thoughtfully, my mind shuffling through so many thoughts at once. I hear Ethan clearly, but his words feel abstract, like trying to touch clouds in the sky.

Still, one thing he said lingers, sticking to me like glue.

"You have a wife?" I ask.

"I'm a widower," he replies evenly. "My family died in a car accident on Laurel Canyon. They were visiting my sister-in-law, stayed too late, and encountered a drunk driver."

"Wow," I say softly, my voice barely above a whisper. How did I not know this? How did I miss such a vital piece of his life on our first date?

The truth hits me hard: I'm selfish. That's the truth —I'm selfish.

"What are you thinking, Sienna?" Ethan's voice pulls me back.

I hadn't realized I'd averted my gaze, staring at the floor without really seeing it. I shake my head, trying to gather my thoughts.

"I should've asked you about your life when I first met you," I admit, my voice trembling. "I wasn't interested in knowing anything about you, I guess. I was selfish."

Ethan leans forward slightly, his tone probing but free of accusation. "What does selfish mean to you?"

My eyebrows shoot up. What kind of question is that? Yet, it's surprisingly provocative.

Ethan waits, his patience steady and unyielding.

"To think only of yourself and not others," I finally reply.

"Is that what you do, Sienna?" His gaze sharpens slightly, though his tone remains calm. "Consider only yourself before others? Because…" He glances at his notepad. "I've heard you say you spent most of your life putting your mother before your own safety and happiness. You put her first when you needed her most."

Did I say that? Maybe. I think I did. His words hit me like a blow to the chest.

Tears stream down my face as I let the memories overtake me—how, through all the chaos, I never considered what I needed.

"She told me my father was dead, you know," I say, my voice trembling. I sniff back the tears as Ethan retrieves a box of tissues from the corner of his desk and hands it to me.

"Thank you," I whisper, taking one before continuing. "She went to jail for thirty days because of her husband at the time—Lieutenant, that was his name. He reported her for stealing three hundred thousand dollars from him, which she did. While she was away, Lieutenant put me out of his shabby little house. I had to take all her stuff with me."

"Were you homeless?" Ethan asks gently.

"Yes. I lived in Rush's car." My throat tightens, and I pause, gathering the strength to continue. "But I never missed a day of school so I could keep those As. I was so hungry. So tired. And yet, I had to focus. Do good. Succeed. And for money, I used my mom's ID to Instacart."

"You were resourceful," Ethan says.

"Always. Even then."

But I'm not done. I have to tell him this. He would be the first person I've ever told.

"But…" I continue, my voice trembling. "I had her things, and I don't know, I think I was searching for an answer—something to explain why my life was so shitty. So I looked through every bit of her stuff, and that's when I found it.

A letter. From my real father. Telling Rush to stay out of his life. He didn't care that I was his."

My lips remain parted as the words hang in the air. My throat tightens further, choking me from the inside. The room feels too small, the air too heavy.

"Breathe, Sienna," Ethan says gently, his voice steady and anchoring. "You've done exceptionally well for our first session. So breathe."

CHAPTER THIRTY-EIGHT

S itting at my desk in the room I set up as my home office, I'm on autopilot, sending out the lecture and case modules I promised my students. The mechanical nature of the task steadies me, but it does nothing to ease the odd, unsettling feeling I've been carrying since my session with Ethan earlier today.

We didn't talk much about Tony—the man who's been the source of my current misery. And yet, somehow, he's moved so far from the forefront of my mind. All I can sense is a glaring vision of Rush. Even as I stare blankly at my computer screen, my thoughts spinning, all I can see is her. Is that good? I don't know. Did Ethan play some Jedi mind trick on me? I don't know that either.

I have another session with him tomorrow afternoon. Part of me doesn't want to show up. But... I have to push myself, because he's left me out here, stripped bare, with nothing to anchor me or cling to.

What I said about Rush felt so raw. It felt wrong—like I was revealing secrets that were only supposed to stay between us. She still hasn't returned my call. The residue of her rejection clings to me, like a heavy, unrelenting sludge in my brain and heart.

I tell myself to let it go. Not to call again. Just wait until she's ready—if she's ever ready.

There. I hit send on the modules. My work is done.

I sit quietly in my chair, my angst swirling in a storm of thoughts about Rush, refusing to settle. My insides rebel against what I want to do next. I glance at my phone, my hand hovering uncertainly.

And then, as if struck by lightning, the truth crashes into me.

Tony has been treating me exactly the way she does.

In my moments of need, when I'm lost in turmoil, desperate for resolution, answers, or even just a shred of empathy, I reach out to them—both of them—and I'm ignored.

Then, when they need something from me, they call. And I—because I'm starved for connection, for validation—take it as an act of love.

Their needs are fulfilled, and mine are left...

What happens to mine?

I don't know.

The realization hits hard and fast. My fingers close around my phone, my hand trembling. My stomach tightens, anticipating rejection.

But I call her anyway.

Three rings. Voicemail.

I call again.

And again.

And again.

And I don't stop.

I won't stop. Until—

"Sienna?" Rush's voice, husky from too many ciga-rettes and sharp with surprise, cuts through the receiver.

My mouth opens, but no words come out. I didn't plan for this moment. I have nothing prepared, and honestly, I don't even know what to say to her. Over the years, I've learned not to trust her with my turmoil. Sometimes I call just to check in, but that's not what this is. Thanksgiving is a few days away. Do I want to spend the holiday with her? Do I ever want to spend it with her? Does she even want to spend it with me?

"Hello," I say finally, my tone hesitant.

"What do you want? You called me." Her voice is harsh, cold.

I shake my head at her bluntness, struggling to find the words. What do I say? What do I even want to say? The first thing that tumbles out is, "Tony and I are not together."

I instantly regret it. Why did I tell her that?

"Uh-huh," she replies, as if she couldn't care less. "Is that it? Is that why you kept calling me like you're crazy? Is that what you wanted to say?"

My stomach tightens. I feel like throwing up. Hanging up on her is a real option—it would be a first. But no. I rally. I open my eyes, determined to push through this conversation and reach something. Maybe mutual respect? It has to exist at some point, doesn't it?

"He found his match with the YPM band. Have you heard of it?"

The silence that follows is unbearable. It stretches far too long, and I can't take it anymore.

"What's wrong with me, for goodness' sake? Why do you hate me so much? I'm your daughter! You carried me in your stomach for nine months, and this is how you treat me? This is how you love me?"

The words pour out of me, raw and unfiltered. My chest heaves. I'm exhausted, weak, as if I have nothing left because I've given her my soul, laid it bare for her to see.

"I have no time for this tonight, Sienna," she finally says, her voice dismissive. "If this is what you called me for…"

Click. I hang up.

She was going to do it first—I could feel it coming. She's done it before. But not tonight.

Tonight, I did it. I hung up on her.

"Bitch," I mutter under my breath, the word slipping out before I can stop it. For once, I don't regret saying it.

TUESDAY NOVEMBER 24, 2099

CHAPTER THIRTY-NINE

The air in Ethan's casita feels heavier as I pace, angry and restless. Sleep evaded me completely last night. I tossed and turned, trapped in a battle of conflicting emotions that seemed insurmountable. I've already told Ethan about all of it—the whirlwind in my head, the aching in my chest.

"As time passed, I wanted to drive to Rush's house and apologize." I halt to look at him. "I even visualized her hugging me, telling me, 'It's okay, darling, I know you love me. I love you too.'" My voice cracks on the last sentence.

Ethan listens silently, his steady gaze fixed on me, grounding me in the truth pressing harder against my heart.

"I couldn't get that scene out of my head," I continue. "I'm a fool. I must be a fool. And it's tragic, really, because if she doesn't love me, and he doesn't love me..." I pause, the realization tearing through me. "Then who does?"

The words hang in the air, heavy and unrelenting. My eyes meet Ethan's, and his unflinching gaze holds steady. The weight of my admission grows unbearable, blooming raw and undeniable.

"She doesn't love me, and that's that. And neither does Tony." My eyes fill with tears, and this time, I don't try to hold them back. I don't try to explain them away or numb them into oblivion.

"Have a seat," Ethan says gently, his voice calm and unwavering. Somehow, in this moment, I trust him completely. After all, he's the one who has expertly guided me to this painful but necessary realization.

I sink into the sofa, a flood of emotions surging within me. I blow my nose, wipe my tears, and wait, my throat too tight to speak.

"As I've already said, you've done excellent work in just two days," Ethan says. "But that's because you're ready. You've hit what I call the emotional bottom. And I promise you, if you stick with this, there's nowhere to go but up."

I nod stiffly, unable to reply. My chest feels like it's caving in.

"Don't fight your true emotions," Ethan whispers. "Let them go."

"Okay," I whimper, the words barely audible.

And then the dam bursts. My tears pour out, followed by deep, primal wailing. I am bawling uncontrollably. For once, I don't stop myself. I don't try to fix myself, to stop the ache. I just let myself be.

CHAPTER FORTY

E than doesn't glance at the clock once during our session, reminding me not to worry about time either. He's calm, patient, and deeply present. As he explains the psyche to me, his words feel like threads unraveling the knots in my mind. He talks about how I might've chosen Tony because he felt familiar.

"If it wasn't Tony," he says, "it likely would've been someone very similar."

To prove his point, he asks me to recount past relationships. With each story I share, I start to see the same pattern: me, practically begging to be loved.

"You remember the night we had dinner," I say.

"Yes," Ethan says, his nod encouraging me to go on.

I squirm against the sofa, my discomfort mounting. I can't believe I want to admit this, but the need to unburden myself burns too strongly to ignore.

"After I left the restaurant, I went to Tony's house… to watch it. I do that a lot. Or I did that a lot." Admitting this secret shame opens the door to more. "Recently, I went into the house while they were on vacation and snooped through Tony's computer. That's how I found out he was with her before he…"

My voice wavers, and I shake my head, squeezing my eyes shut against the truth I already know. "He was with her before he gifted me a YPM band. They were already attached, already intimate, and that revelation? It wasn't enough to make me stop yearning for him."

Ethan leans back, observing me carefully. "What if Tony had been completely honest with you from the start? What would you have done?"

I SHAKE MY HEAD, STRUGGLING TO IMAGINE TONY saying, *"I'm going to wear the YPM and see if I have a quantum match, whether you like it or not."*

But that's exactly what he had done.

Ethan's voice interrupts my spiraling thoughts. "What about your mother? What if she had told you the truth?"

I frown, confused. "Rush? What if she told me the truth about what?"

Ethan tilts his head slightly, his gaze steady and unflinching. "What if she said: *Sienna, I couldn't love you the way you deserve to be loved. No, I don't care that you're divorced. I don't feel like a mother because I always come first. You're on your own, so stop wanting something I can't give you. But when I need you, I want you right here—at my beck and call.*"

My eyes widen, and my breath catches.

Is that Rush's voice?

Yes. It is.

I fight the urge to bat away everything Ethan just said, to shove it into the furthest corners of my mind. But I can't.

Rush does always come first. When I need her, she's never there. I'm going through all these trials with Tony completely alone.

A lump forms in my throat, tightening until it feels impossible to swallow.

I want to cry, but I also want to take this truth like an adult, to bear it without breaking.

Barely breathing, I whisper, "Oh... That truth."

"You acknowledge that's your mother's voice?" Ethan asks gently.

"Yes," I manage to say, my voice barely audible.

"Does her voice sound like someone else you vowed to be close to?"

I nod stiffly, tears streaming down my face.

"And listen, Sienna, about lurking on your husband's property—you know that's wrong?"

"Of course," I reply with a repentant sigh.

"There's no need to shame yourself for it—it's done. But if you find yourself in that place again, try reasoning your way out using the tools we've discussed in our sessions. And if that doesn't work, call me. I won't judge you, and we'll talk it through. Okay?"

"Okay," I manage to say.

But as soon as the word leaves my lips, a wave of intense loss crashes over me, hollowing me out. It feels as though Tony is now, and forever, gone.

And yet, a question bubbles to the surface, one I

can't suppress. "What did you do when you lost your family?" I blurt, the words escaping before I can stop them.

It's a bold question, and I instantly regret it. But here he is, sitting across from me—a whole, unbroken man. I want what he has. If it's possible for me to have it.

Ethan's lips tighten, holding back a flood of unspoken grief. "A lot of hard work, Sienna. Reality-based work. It starts with accepting that sometimes life ends early. Sometimes life ends late."

"I'm sorry if I overstepped," I say quietly.

He waves my apology away. "No, it's fine. It still hurts sometimes to talk about it. It's hard to believe a whole family can be... gone. Their laughs. The feel of my wife Ray's cheek against my lips." He looks away briefly, gathering himself. "She was my best friend."

"But you wore the YPM band," I say cautiously.

"I did."

"Then... you're ready for love?"

He snorts softly, a small smile tugging at the corners of his lips as he shakes his head, momentarily shedding his therapist persona. "I don't know, Sienna. I was shocked that I even came up with a match."

His eyes glisten with unshed tears as he pauses. "When I think about the technology—how it's essentially powered by the energy our bodies emit—I was stunned to learn I could even be matched again after Ray."

I hesitate, almost too afraid to ask my next question. But curiosity wins. "Has your support ticket turned up your true match?"

Ethan lets out a soft chuckle, shaking his head. "Not yet. But if it does, I'd be the luckiest man in the world. And if it doesn't? I'd still be the luckiest man alive. Because I've loved and been loved, unconditionally. Most people live a lifetime and never experience that."

THURSDAY, NOVEMBER 26, 2099
THANKSGIVING DAY

CHAPTER FORTY-ONE

W hat does one do when a habit is etched into her bones? Today is Thanksgiving, and I'm trying my hardest to treat it like any other regular day.

Last year, I spent the holiday with Tony's family and friends at our house—what used to be our house. The food was catered, and a soul band played all the top hits. Everyone had a great time. But during our wedding reception, I faded into the background, finding a quiet table where I nursed a single glass of wine and watched the festivities unfold. It felt like I was watching a movie, a scene I never thought would be written for me.

The Swift is running on its regular schedule today, but the city feels deserted. There are only six other passengers onboard besides me. My exit—the one where I'd get off to walk to Tony's house—is just four stops away.

It's been two days since my last session with Ethan,

yet here I am, planning something so emotionally unstable.

It wasn't easy getting to this moment. Everything I've uncovered about my mother and Tony churns in my mind. Tuesday night was sleepless, a storm of inward cringing as I realized, again and again, how alike they are—my mother and my husband, two halves of the same coin.

I'm moving out of my apartment—well, Tony's apartment since he's the legal lessee. But the move isn't optional anymore. Tony didn't pay his share of the rent as promised, nor did he charm Demetria into giving me any leniency. She made it clear: if the balance isn't paid by the 30th, the eviction process begins.

Before hopping on the Swift, I was packing. Carefully folding my clothes into plastic containers, I told myself I could just leave. I'm not legally obligated to pay. But when I spoke to Demetria earlier, I assured her I'd take care of it by tomorrow.

Now, I'm not sure I should. Especially after learning the lease is month-to-month—a fact Tony conveniently hid. He claimed it was a year-long lease. He lied. Again.

I could do something entirely unlike me—just leave and let the chips fall where they may.

But as I packed, the loneliness of the day hit me like a tsunami. Memories of last year's holiday celebration flooded in, and the thought of what must be happening at Tony's house right now consumed me. I couldn't stop picturing it—family, friends, Tanya—all gathered in a scene of joy I'm no longer a part of.

Without a second thought, ignoring every tool Ethan

gave me, I grabbed my coat, slung my purse over my shoulder, and headed out the door.

And now here I am, on the Swift, gliding through a chilly afternoon under gray, looming clouds. After a smoldering summer, I usually welcome the cold. But today, the chill feels heavier, like it's seeped into my bones. I can't tell if it's the weather or the weight of what I'm about to do.

Deep down, I don't want to do this. I don't want to stand in those itchy hedges, peering into Tony's house, watching them smile and pretend their lives are perfect.

When the train stops at my destination, I remain seated, immovable as a boulder.

I don't need to know.

I don't want to know.

Yes, I want to be part of a scene like Tony creates—joyful, warm, alive. But I don't want to be a spectator of the Tony show anymore. I want something real, something mine.

Just to be safe, I ride to the next stop, get off, and cross under the tunnel to take the train back in the opposite direction.

I'm going home.

When I get there, I'll shut the blinds, lock the world out, and let sleep take me. Let this day fade into the void where it belongs. Tomorrow, I'll find the strength to begin again.

But just as I settle into my seat on the returning train, my phone buzzes with a message.

I glance down.

It's from Lena.

Lena Chest, Department Head: 4:37 PM

Hey Sienna! If you're not doing anything today, there's a spot at our table for you! Dinner is this evening at seven. Best, Lena.

My heart instantly feels lighter, as if it's floating toward the tomorrow I've just envisioned. Before I can type out my reply to Lena, a voice pulls me from my thoughts.

"Professor Holloway?"

I glance up from my phone, ready to respond, but I hesitate. I almost correct him—technically, I'm a lecturer, not a professor—but stop myself. Why diminish the acknowledgment? I'm always doing that, knocking myself off a pedestal or two unless it's indisputably mine. But my students see me as their professor, and in this moment, that's exactly who I am to this man.

As I take a closer look, his face comes into focus. Those bright, naturally curious eyes jog my memory. He's one of my former students. I remember thinking he seemed like a kid back when he sat in my class two or three years ago. But maybe it's me. Now that I'm thirty-one, anyone south of twenty-five looks like a kid, even though he's probably not much younger than I am.

"Yes, it is you," he says, his face lighting up like he's just found a pearl in an oyster.

And then, his name surfaces in my mind. "Waagosh," I say. He was the only Native student I've ever taught. Ojibwe.

"Yes," he replies, delighted that I remember him.

"Look…" He glances ahead as the train barrels forward. "My stop is next, but it's funny I ran into you—I've always wanted to thank you."

"Oh," I reply, completely caught off guard. "Well, you're welcome."

His smile broadens, his gaze softening as it sweeps over my face. "No, really, Professor Holloway, you changed the trajectory of my life. I forced myself to excel through traditional American education institutions, swallowing the bitter taste of them, until I got to your class. Your teaching style resonated with me. Those modules where you made us rewrite laws and policies according to our belief systems—while staying within legal boundaries but finding loopholes for change—that's why I am where I am today."

I give him a curious once-over, eager to hear the answer to my next question. "And where is that?" I ask.

"I'm an international environmental rights lawyer."

I sit up straighter, genuinely impressed. "Wow."

HE GLANCES OUT THE WINDOW IMPATIENTLY AS THE Swift approaches the slow zone. "Yeah. Listen…" He reaches into his coat pocket and pulls out a sleek silver card holder. "Our firm is always looking for talented lawyers who think outside the box. We should talk."

The Swift stops, and the doors hiss open. I take the card, offering a polite smile, though the idea of a career change doesn't sit well with me. Even with the looming reality that I won't have a job at the end of the quarter, my resistance feels tied to something deeper. Pride, maybe? A student offering me a job feels like a subtle jab —a reminder of how stuck I've been. Trapped in an emotionally devastating marriage and a job I can barely execute with the passion and inspiration I once had.

I think of his words, how my teaching changed his trajectory, and I wonder about the version of myself— the one he remembers so fondly. How did that person fade into this shadow I hardly recognize? I'm sure he hasn't seen my latest course reviews. If he had, would he still be offering me this opportunity? And honestly, how in the world could I ever become an "international environmental rights lawyer"? It feels like a job from another lifetime—one far removed from where I am now.

"Okay," I say, forcing a grateful smile. "Thank you." I let him see me tuck the card into my purse.

"Good," he says, stepping toward the open doors. "It was a pleasure seeing you, Professor Holloway. I hope one day we can become colleagues." With that, he steps onto the platform, giving a quick wave as the train begins to accelerate toward the rapid tube.

I glance down at the business card tucked neatly in my purse. I can't let myself think about it right now—it's too much, too soon. Instead, I pull out my phone and see Lena's message still waiting. Her offer feels like a lifeline, a way to ground myself, even if only for a few hours.

Without hesitation, I tap out a reply:

4:48 PM

Thank you for the offer. I'll be there!

Lena doesn't disappoint. Within a minute, my phone buzzes with her reply:

> Lena Chest, Department Head: 4:49
>
> Great! We can't wait to see you. Bring your appetite and your charm!

I can't stop smiling. Charming? Humph. The thought makes me chuckle softly to myself. For the first time all day, a small sense of certainty washes over me. At least now, I know where I'm going after I head home to shower and make myself presentable. I actually have plans—real plans—with people who want me there.

It's a small step, but it feels significant, like I'm finally placing a foot in the right direction. A part of me still aches with uncertainty, but for the first time in a long while, I feel like I'm moving forward.

CHAPTER FORTY-TWO

TONY

"**N**obody stays in town for Thanksgiving," Tanya said last week when I suggested hosting a dinner party at my house. There wouldn't have been an expensive band, but I still had enough disposable cash to hire Golden Torch Catering, the best in the city. My friends, family, and close colleagues had been texting and calling, asking when their invitations would arrive. I always send messenger invites to each guest, a tradition people seemed to love.

Needless to say, Vonita and Reign weren't thrilled when I told them Tanya and I would be traveling this year instead. My friends weren't happy either. Rebecca even told me, "You've changed since Tanya came into the picture—and not for the better."

Whatever.

Now, here I am in St. Barthélemy, regretting the decision. I should've stuck to my guns. Hosting Thanksgiving dinner at my house is a tradition. I even tried convincing Tanya, telling her, "Dinner at my house is important. Plus, we've already spent a lot of money traveling."

Her response still echoes in my head. She was in the other room, probably lounging in bed. I couldn't see her, but I knew she was naked, her sensually round hips draped in our damp sheets from making love. Her voice drifted out, teasing and sharp. "Are you complaining about money, Tony?"

I froze mid-shave, razor in hand, the blade hovering over the edge of my jaw. Hell, I *was* complaining about money, but I didn't think I'd been obvious about it.

"Because Alexander Creston would never complain about paying for a little old one- or two-day trip—well, four days because we'll take the weekend—to St. Barts," she added, her tone saccharine sweet.

I seethed, gripping my razor tighter. Why the hell did she have to mention him? It was cruel. Tanya knows his name is a hot-button word for me. It felt like she'd just driven a needle straight into my pride.

But it worked because I gave in.

At least I didn't have to buy our plane tickets—the hosts covered that, first class too. Chandler Strauss clearly has a lot of money, and he enjoys spreading it around, making sure everyone knows it. That's fine by me; I haven't spent much on food or accommodations either. We're staying in a villa perched on the cliffside of Chandler's sprawling estate, and I have to admit, the views are spectacular.

Still, Tanya keeps baiting me, making sideways comments about Chandler and the people he knows. She brings up their history—how they dated once—but brushes it off like it's ancient news. Yet her tone makes me think she's waiting for a reaction.

I don't like being baited into jealousy.

I don't have a problem with Chandler. I know guys like him. He's simple. He likes money, he likes status, and he loves women. And that's that. He's not a commitment guy, never will be. Other than the fact that he once slept with Tanya—which I now have very well covered—he's not a threat to me.

Now, we're all gathered for dinner, fifteen of us seated at one long table. It's not how I would've arranged it, but to each his own. Chandler sits at one end of the table, his girlfriend Amber at the other. They don't act like a real couple, but that's none of my business. Apparently, they decided to "mix things up," which is why Tanya is seated next to Chandler.

And she's leaning in close to him, laughing softly, touching his arm, whispering something. I wonder what she's saying.

I try to focus on my plate, telling myself not to care. Tanya thrives on this—keeping me on edge is her favorite game.

"So, Anthony," Amber says, cutting into my thoughts. I'm forced to tear my glare away from the show Tanya's putting on for me. She's laying it on thick tonight, her antics clearly aimed at provoking me. I know how this goes: she's angling for one of our infamous jealousy-fueled fights that ends in hate-fueled sex. But tonight, it's not playful—it feels degrading.

"You and Tanya are quantum matches, right?"

Amber asks, settling into her oversized chair like she's holding court.

"Uh-huh," I mutter, hoping she gets to her point quickly.

"I thought it was Your Perfect Match," another voice interjects.

I turn toward the speaker, a petite woman with sleek black hair pulled high into a bun. Her angular face and large, expressive eyes make her look striking. She's sexy.

"The wristband is called YPM," another guest clarifies, holding up their own band for emphasis.

If I decide to stick around, I might bother learning their names.

"Oh my God, you're looking for your perfect match, Randy?" someone teases, and the table erupts into laughter.

So that guy's name is Randy. Got it.

"Why not? It worked for Tanya," Randy quips, leaning back with a smirk. Then, out of nowhere, he adds, "Remember how she used to sniff around Chandler's ass like a horny dog?"

Amber gasps, pretending to be scandalized but clearly entertained. "Stop it," she says, her grin betraying her amusement.

And Tanya?

She smiles that sly, calculated smile she gets when she's about to deliver a sharp retort. "I'm not sniffing his ass ever again," she says, her tone playful but biting. Then, with a casual shrug that twists the knife, she adds, "The universe gave me Tony's perfect ass to sniff, and it smells way better."

The table bursts into laughter.

Am I supposed to join in?

I don't find any of it funny—not at all. Maybe I should. Maybe I'm just being uptight since James dropped off the radar. Maybe that's why I'm struggling to get into the social atmosphere in general.

The last update I got about James's whereabouts was from Collin and Teague, two guys he often had lunch with. They both said he went back to San Francisco because of a family emergency.

Neither of them knows how to get in touch with him, but they promised to let me know as soon as they hear from him. I don't believe them, but I can't force them to tell me the truth—they're not on my team.

"So, what do you have?" the cute girl with the high hair and angelic face asks, her gaze locking onto mine with an intensity that feels more like a challenge than a question.

"What do you mean?" I grumble, trying to keep my irritation at Tanya's behavior from showing.

"Is it a permanent match…" Her eyes narrow, a teasing smirk forming. Just as her voice dips, sultry and low, she adds, "Or is it temporary?"

"It's permanent, Alice," Tanya cuts in, her voice slicing through the air like a whip. She raises her hand deliberately, the overpriced engagement ring I bought her glinting obnoxiously under the overhead lights. "So back the hell up."

A-lee-ch-e. That's how Tanya pronounced her name.

I swallow hard, startled by Tanya's outburst. I've never seen her do anything like that before. It's obvious she doesn't like this girl. But something happens in that moment. My gaze shifts back to *A-lee-ch-e*, and an image flashes in my mind: her beneath me, her body arching, my hands gripping her hips as I sink myself inside her. *Ooh, that feels good.*

The vision jolts me—vivid and unexpected—and, for the first time in a long while, I feel something new. Something different. It's as if Tanya's allure is finally starting to fade, and not a moment too soon. Look at her: shouting profanities across the table, territorial and tactless. She's practically daring Chandler to take her. Normally, this would be the moment I start crafting my excuse to leave this Thanksgiving minibreak—to escape this shabby group of so-called friends, who seem to have no loyalty to one another, and let Tanya carry on with whatever quest she's on to fuck the host.

But I won't leave.

I'll stay. Thanks to *A-lee-ch-e*.

I'm staying.

FRIDAY, NOVEMBER 27, 2099

CHAPTER FORTY-THREE

I hear the ding of a message and the familiar buzz of my phone. What time is it? I didn't get home until almost midnight last night. Dinner with Lena's family and friends turned out to be the best Thanksgiving I've ever had. We played Charades and a game I'd never heard of before, called *Heads Up*. In it, you guess the word on the card on your forehead using clues from others before the timer runs out. Later, we settled in with glasses of expensive, delicious wine as Leo led the most thought-provoking conversations about the world we live in—its past, present, and the future we all envisioned.

It was perfect. And, unexpectedly, I made some new friends.

When I finally went to bed, I felt relaxed. I tried so hard to care about whatever Tony and Tanya might have been doing for the holiday, but I couldn't summon the will to think about them for more than a fleeting second. Something is happening to me. I don't know exactly what it is, but it feels like I'm being haunted by a future that hasn't yet arrived—a future that's brighter, lighter, and filled with promise. Some might call it optimism.

My phone buzzes again, jolting me out of my thoughts. Another message. Whoever's texting me isn't about to stop.

I don't reach for it right away. Instead, with my blankets pulled tightly around me, I glance around my room. My eyes land on the stack of packed boxes neatly lined up against the walls.

Why are they still there?

Why am I still here?

The surge of optimism I felt just moments ago suddenly dips, leaving an empty void in its place. It's not doom, exactly. It's... nothing. A numbness I can't quite shake.

Finally, I reach for my phone.

Sitting up against the headboard, I glance at the screen.

The messages are from Rush.

Rush: 9:37 AM

I'm not a monster. It gets hard for me. I try. I tried with you. I'm just no good at being a mom. That's why I only had one, you. And I shouldn't have done that.

My head feels light, almost disconnected, as I pull my eyes away from the screen. For the first time, I've read the unvarnished truth from my mother: she regrets having me. Deep down, I've always known this. She's shown it in countless ways.

Once, I read somewhere—though I can't remember where—that it doesn't matter why or how we were brought into this world. What matters is that we survive and understand we belong to ourselves. It's our responsibility to build a life worth living.

I let the words sink in as I take stock of my emotions. Do her words hurt? Very little. They don't sting the way I once imagined they would. Instead, they feel like confirmation—a truth I've carried quietly for years. There's nothing left to feel about it.

I'm ready to read the rest.

Rush: 9:39 AM

Heath and I got into a fight yesterday. He's in jail. You think you can loan me bail? I'll pay you back.

I think I'm going to invest in one of those YPM bands. I can do better than him.

I stare at the message, my thumb hovering over the screen. The audacity—asking for money while casually mentioning that she's already considering trading Heath in for someone better, as if swapping out one broken appliance for a shinier model is no big deal. And then there's the part about the YPM band, which is definitely not cheap.

Flames flash through me, quick and hot, like a lighter struck against dry air. Anger.

Normally, I'd put my phone face down and look away, running from this anger, burying it beneath a mountain of denial. By the day's end, I'd have pushed it out of my mind entirely, filing her words away with all the others I've ignored over the years: her disregard, her unloving expectations.

But not today.

Today, I sit with the fire. I let it burn, refusing to run from the uncomfortable truth smoldering inside me. In her mind, she doesn't have a daughter. She has a servant. A dumpster for her guilt and failures. Someone to clean up her messes while asking for nothing in return.

And so, there's only one answer she needs to hear.

My fingers move across the screen—steady, deliberate.

> 9:51 AM
>
> No.

I press Send and block her number without hesitation. I may never unblock her. And that's okay—at least, I think it is. I'll have to ask Ethan.

TUEDAY, DECEMBER 1, 2099

CHAPTER FORTY-FOUR

My session with Ethan began promptly at 6:00 p.m., and I didn't waste a second diving into the whirlwind of my week. I told him why I've been feeling so flustered: I officially moved out of Tony's apartment on Monday.

"I hired movers," I said, crossing one leg over the other as I settled into the chair. "Made the whole thing less of a hassle."

I moved back to Pasadena, which, despite the chaos, feels like a homecoming. A rental search turned up a guesthouse not far from where I used to live. It's perfect —nestled in a neighborhood of tree-lined streets where the houses retain their classic charm. The kind of place where modernization stops at the essentials: upgraded sewer lines, built-in solar panels, and temperature-responsive crystalline paneling.

"I like it there," I told Ethan. "It's quaint and comforting, like stepping back into a life that makes sense."

Of course, the move hasn't been without its challenges. Boxes are stacked everywhere, and the sheer amount of unpacking ahead is daunting. "I'm exhausted," I admitted, "but I can't stop yet. There's too much to do before I can even think about resting."

Ethan listened intently, nodding in his quiet, patient way, before gently steering the conversation toward something heavier. That's when I updated him on my final communications with Rush.

"And so, yes," I say to Ethan with a flustered, unsure sigh, one that comes from the deepest parts of me—the parts that despise the relationship I have with my mother. "That's how I chose to handle Rush."

He grunts thoughtfully, leaning back in his chair. "I'm going to ask you a very complex question—are you ready?"

I sit up straighter, bracing myself for a question that might somehow knock me off this newfound sense of balance I think I've found. "Yes. I'm ready."

He sets his pen and notepad down on the desk, his full attention shifting to me. "Is there any scenario you can imagine where you could've made a decision about how to proceed with your mother that would have resulted in mutual regard, self-respect, and healthy satisfaction?"

"No," I reply without hesitation. "I know that because I've asked myself those questions in one form or another, and I keep coming up with the same answer. Rush is Rush, and I can't do our relationship the way she needs it anymore."

His smile is small but warm—satisfied, maybe even a little proud. "That sounds healthy to me."

"Then why do I feel like I slapped her in the face several times on one hand, and like I've finally protected my heart on the other?"

Ethan grunts thoughtfully, his brows knitting together as he gives my question some serious consideration.

"You don't stop loving your mother because you're falling into nurturing love with yourself," Ethan says at last. "You don't even have to stop being in an active relationship with your mother to advocate for yourself. You merely have a line, Sienna. And your mother has a choice. She can either stay on the side where she stands today, and you'll love her from a distance. Or she can operate within the spectrum of your boundaries and join you on your side of the line.

"During our future sessions, you'll learn about boundaries: what they are, how to set them, and, most importantly, how to enforce them."

I inhale deeply, his words resonating within me. That was profound. For the first time in a long time, I feel something glowing intensely inside me—optimism.

A smile quirks at my lips. "So... is this why they pay you the big bucks?"

Ethan roars with laughter, a hearty laugh I've come to appreciate. It roots him somehow, anchoring him as a stabilizing figure in my life. And he's happy.

"It's not always this easy," he says, his smile lingering. "Most clients want to hold onto what they have. They expect everyone around them to change so they can be happy. They don't come to me to heal themselves —they want me to fix everyone else.

"But in your case, nothing around you was left standing. You knew it was you that had to change. So you needed to trust me completely. Does that make sense?"

"Yes," I say breathlessly. It makes perfect sense. So much so that I'm finally ready to admit something else.

"On Thanksgiving, I wanted to see him and her, living what I thought was the life I was missing out on. So, I boarded a Swift and headed to Tony's house. But the longer I sat on that train, the clearer I saw myself. I realized what I was doing. And I knew it wasn't worth it. So… I stayed on the train."

I pause, the memory warming me now.

"And on the way home, ready to have a boring, lonely Thanksgiving, two things happened: Lena messaged me with an invitation—which I've already told you about—and I ran into a former student who thanked me for being an effective professor."

"Oh?" Ethan prompts, his tone encouraging, inviting me to elaborate.

The memory of Waagosh makes me smile. "He gave me his business card, inviting me to join his firm. Can you believe that? A former student offered me a job." I chuckle softly at the irony.

"And what's wrong with that?"

I open my mouth to respond but hesitate, distracted. I've been staring at Ethan, trying to figure out what's different about him. Did he grow out his hair? Lose weight? Spend a day at a spa? Something's changed.

"How have you been?" I ask suddenly, blurting out the question that's been nagging me. Because I see it now—he's glowing. Radiating. I'm sure I'm not imagining this. "Because you look amazing."

His smile widens, and he nods, glancing off to the side as if picturing whatever's causing his happiness. "I've been really good."

I tilt my head, too curious to let it drop. "Why have you been really good?"

"Well…" He pauses for effect, his eyes sparkling with a contagious joy I can't ignore. "My help ticket was resolved. Quantum Matching fixed the error, and I have a match."

My jaw drops. That's why he's glowing. And to my surprise, I recognize the glow—it's the same one Tony wore for weeks before presenting me with a YPM band.

Ethan watches me closely, then adds, "I asked if they resolved your false match as well. Initially, they didn't want to give me any information about your case. But I assured them I'm your new therapist and—"

"No way," I cut him off, shaking my head vehemently. I wave my hands like I'm trying to swat the very idea out of the air. "My heart and mind need a huge break after Tony, who was… actually is truly awful."

"Wounded," Ethan corrects gently. "Tony is wounded. And you know, we're all wounded, but that doesn't mean we can't find steady, healthy love."

I groan and sigh, shaking my head again. Frankly, I don't want to talk about me. I'm too curious about him. "Not yet. Maybe one day. But… so… you've actually met your match?"

His face lights up again. "Yes. I have."

"And? Did you experience it? The fireworks?"

He nods, his expression turning thoughtful, as if he's reliving the moment. "It was more than fireworks."

"Then it's real?"

"Very much so."

Suddenly, my sinuses swell, and tears sting my eyes. Every fiber of my being rejects what Ethan's experience might offer me. I can't stop shaking my head, as if denying the very possibility of it for myself. "You must understand, Ethan," I say, my voice cracking. "I'm just so beaten and battered…" I press both hands over my heart, stacking them as if to shield it from further harm. "…in here."

"I know, Sienna," Ethan says gently. "I'm not pushing you to meet your match. You'll do it on your own terms, if you're ever ready. But I want you to reflect on something."

My eyebrows lift, silently urging him to continue.

"It's not your match that you're rebuffing. It's the feeling of being safe. Allowing unconditional love into your life."

He picks up a computer notebook from his desk, taps on the screen a few times, and then turns it toward me. "For instance... this."

I squint at the screen, recognizing what looks like a financial worksheet. My eyes catch on a figure: $900—the amount I've paid him for our sessions.

"I've refunded you the amount. I meant what I said," Ethan continues. "I'm offering our sessions without charge. What I'm giving you is unconditional support. Look at your boss, Lena—she invited you to dinner with her family, out of unconditional friendship. You're already letting unconditional people into your life. So think about how that feels. Really ask yourself: do you want more of us in your orbit?"

Fighting back tears, I give a sharp, silent nod. "Thank you."

The silence stretches between us, heavy and meaningful.

"You think I'll ever be ready for love without conditions?" I finally ask, my voice barely above a whisper. The thought of loving again still feels impossibly distant.

"Yes. I do," he says without hesitation. His voice is steady and sure, and I love that about him. "You keep working on your boundaries, and pretty soon, as they say, the wheat will separate from the chaff."

I nod slowly, swallowing the lump forming in my throat.

Ethan glances at his watch and shifts gears. "Now, we've got eighteen minutes left. Let's dig more into boundaries."

WEDNESDAY, DECEMBER 2, 2099

CHAPTER FORTY-FIVE

I'm right on time for class today, and for the first time in a long while, it feels right. Really right. I spent every spare moment before this lecture preparing, organizing, and focusing. After yesterday's session with Ethan, I couldn't stop ruminating on Waagosh's offer and the realization that struck me like lightning: my students are my colleagues. There's no power dynamic here.

I used to know that instinctively—before Tony came into my life and made me feel small. With him, I was always clawing for recognition, scratching for a sliver of equality. Most of the time, I failed. And every time I failed, he made me feel like my life choices were mediocre, insignificant, unremarkable.

But something shifts as I look out over the faces in front of me now. Yes, there's a noticeable dent in attendance. A quarter of my students have dropped out of this class, leaving empty seats like ghosts of my mistakes. Before my demise, I packed classrooms. Students would stand through entire sessions just to be part of my lectures. I never appreciated it back then—never paused to take pride in the significance of it.

But I'm doing it now.

I look at the ones who stayed, who stuck with me, and my chest swells with gratitude so raw it threatens to burst. My eyes fill with tears, but I refuse to let them fall. They don't deserve my breakdown; they deserve my best.

"Good morning," I say, breaking the silence.

Their response is a halfhearted murmur, a sound that echoes exhaustion and survival. That's okay. I understand. They're hanging on, just like I've been doing.

I step out from behind the lectern, moving to the front of the room where I can see them more clearly.

"I have a story to tell you," I say, my voice steady but warm. I take a deep breath. Here goes everything.

"Once upon a time, there lived a princess named...well, me." I pat my chest and wink.

That gets their attention. Heads lift. There's even a ripple of low laughter.

"On New Year's Day, at exactly 12:01 a.m., this princess said, 'I do,' to her prince. Only... the prince turned out to be an arrogant, self-centered asshole who couldn't stop prancing in front of mirrors."

The room chuckles again, this time louder.

"He left the princess, and she descended into the depths of despair. But here's the thing." I raise a finger, pausing for emphasis. "She got help. And now she's standing before you, apologizing for being a shitty lecturer. But guess what?"

I take another deep breath, letting the silence settle. Then, I raise my fists high, clenching them like I'm summoning every ounce of strength I have. "She's back!"

The response shocks me. The room erupts. Students clap, some even standing, their energy infusing me with a confidence I haven't felt in ages.

And then, I get to work.

Today, I don't just lecture—I teach. I deliver a session that will go down in the history books, not because I'm extraordinary, but because I finally remembered that I am.

CHAPTER FORTY-SIX

I shared my fairytale story with every class I taught today, and each group gave me the same incredible response as the last. By the time my 3:00 p.m. class rolled around, a few students from earlier sessions had slipped in, eager to hear it again. Word must've spread through the department after my 9:00 a.m. lecture.

It's funny how unalone I feel now, how connected I am to this moment.

I could see it on their faces—the genuine happiness they felt, not just for me but for themselves, for the department as a whole. It was as though my honesty, my vulnerability, had reminded them of something bigger than the daily grind of readings, briefs, and exams.

Today, I wasn't just a lecturer—I was a symbol of why they applied to UCLA in the first place. Why they fought so hard to be here, in these hallowed halls. I was showing them—reminding them—why this is a top-tier law school and why they belong here. And for the first time in a long time, I felt like I belonged here too.

Nearly running down the hallway, I slow as I approach Lena's office.

"Hey, Sienna," her assistant Ray says, her friendly eyes beaming at me.

"Is she in?" I ask, pointing at Lena's door.

"Yeah, but she's about to leave."

I would've let that stop me before. So formal. So careful to keep things professional since Lena is my boss. But now, I've had Thanksgiving with her, for goodness' sake. We're friends—or at least, I'll know where I stand if she puts me in my place.

"That's okay," I say. "I just have something to say to her real quick."

Ray quickly picks up the phone to announce my arrival. Almost instantly, I hear Lena's voice from inside her office. The door swings open, and there she is—dressed in a chic black skirt suit, her impeccably styled bob catching the fluorescent light. She greets me with a dazzling smile.

"Sienna, come in!" she exclaims warmly.

My heart leaps in my chest. I feel... well... accepted. She and I are friends.

I take a seat without waiting for her prompting, making myself comfortable without feeling as if I'm crossing a line. That's why I'm brave enough to say, "Lena, I want to keep my job. And I want to do what-ever it takes to become a full-fledged professor."

Lena jumps to her feet, pumping her fist in the air. "Yes!" she shouts victoriously. "That's all I ever wanted to hear from you. I wanted to see you fight for your job, Sienna!"

The tension drains from my shoulders as I laugh. Lena beams at me, and before I know it, we're hugging —a rare but genuine moment of connection.

We sink back into our seats, and hours pass as I unload everything I've been carrying. I tell Lena about Tony, the whirlwind of emotions, Ethan, and how he's helped me navigate my cloudy era.

Lena listens intently, her sharp eyes soft with understanding. Then, with a mischievous grin, she asks, "Is this Ethan guy still single?"

I laugh, shaking my head. "I never would've looked twice at a guy like him before. But if he were single, I'd probably ask him to dinner. Unfortunately, he's already found his match."

"Ooh," Lena says, rubbing her palms together. "The plot thickens."

"Yeah," I say, exhaling deeply. "He refers to her as his Perfect Match."

At that, Lena's brow arches, her playful tone tinged with mock seriousness. "Oh, no. We definitely don't want to mess with those Perfect Match types."

We both laugh, the kind of laugh that feels like letting go.

Lena drums her fingers on her desk, shifting the conversation. "So, what about Christmas? Got any plans?"

I grin, already knowing where this is going.

"No," I admit, my smile widening.

"Perfect," she says, leaning back in her chair. "You're

coming to my place. Friends, family, plenty of food—and a few eligible bachelors for you to choose from."

Her tone is light, teasing, but she's serious. I can see it in her eyes. She's not letting me spend Christmas alone.

"I accept your invitation. Although, I'll probably decline dating an eligible bachelor for a while. I'm still afraid of my picker. I want to sharpen my discernment first."

"Oh... Is that Ethan's influence again?"

I chuckle. "Yes, it is."

"Are you sure he's not your match?"

"I'm positive. You should see him. He's glowing."

"And you said he initiated a help ticket, right?"

"Uh-huh," I say tightly, knowing exactly where this is leading. Believe it or not, I've thought about it extensively since yesterday's session.

"And did you win a match out of it too?"

I close my eyes as if feeling the impact of her question. Yep, this was what I was expecting.

"He said something," I confess. "But..."

Lena's eyes widen with excitement and far too much encouragement. "But?"

"I'm just so... I need..." I scratch behind my ear, searching for the right words. I don't want to say that I'm broken—it feels cruel, even if it's true.

Ethan likes to call it wounded. Should I say that? Or maybe it's simpler than that.

"I need time," I finally say. "I'm not ready, yet."

Lena hums as she nods, mulling over my claim. "Maybe next year?"

"Maybe," I reply, as if that's some sort of consolation.

"And Sienna," she says softly, leaning forward, "love can be healing. True, healthy love can be healing. So, think about that as you wait to heal yourself—whether or not it's with your Perfect Match."

MONDAY, DECEMBER 14, 2099

CHAPTER FORTY-SEVEN

W inter break has officially begun.

Last year on this very day, I was on cloud nine, only weeks away from marrying the love of my life—or so I thought. Me, Sienna Charles, being proposed to? It was something I'd never imagined, let alone picturing myself as the center of attention at a wedding ceremony.

But here's the funny thing: even though there's no looming wedding, no picture-perfect marriage, I'm still floating on cloud nine.

Each day since I started therapy with Ethan has been better than the last. My mind feels clearer, my heart lighter. The haze that used to weigh down my days is lifting. I'm finally breathing again—really breathing.

We've even reduced my sessions to once a week, every Tuesday. It's progress—the kind I wasn't sure I'd ever make. And it feels good. So good.

That's why I've exited the Swift on Hill Street and 3rd in downtown LA and decided to walk. I'm headed to the Optima Center on Temple Street—the tower that houses businesses committed to global progress, optimism, and community. Today is a green marker air day, and I want to savor it.

Green marker days mean the air quality is so clean you'd hardly believe this city once had some of the worst air pollution in the country. I can't wait for tonight; the skies will be so clear I'll sit out on my patio and stargaze —especially in my neighborhood. Gratitude fills me for that and everything else in my life that's starting to feel aligned.

So, why the Optima Center? That's where Meridian Legal Alliance is headquartered—the law firm that employs Waagosh.

Last week, Waagosh sent me a follow-up email after our conversation. I'd gracefully declined his invitation to work for his firm, thinking I was content with my current path. But Waagosh, ever the lawyer, replied the next day with a carefully crafted argument extolling the firm's mission and values.

He explained how Meridian tackles the grunt work of the law—the kind that doesn't make lawyers multimillionaires but drives real societal change. He emphasized how they're funded by a lucrative trust, enabling them to hire brilliant minds while paying well above industry standards for impact litigation.

He convinced me to join a videoconference call with the partners, and it went swimmingly. For two hours, we discussed how my expertise could benefit their firm. By the end of the day, they made me a compelling offer: an advisory role with three times my teaching salary and far fewer hours. It sounded almost too good to be true.

Today, I'm meeting the partners in person. The crisp air and clear sky mirror my mood as I walk, feeling lighter and more optimistic with each step. This meeting is the final step to solidify the deal.

The sound of my new phone ringing stops me mid-stride. I'd purchased it recently as part of my effort to cut off any contact with my mother. My top priority had been changing my number, ensuring she couldn't reach me—whether through her own calls or by enlisting neighbors I wouldn't recognize.

Tony hadn't crossed my mind in this context. He made it abundantly clear he was done with us. His response to my proposed settlement terms was cold and dismissive, offering me nothing. I don't feel like fighting him, but I also refuse to walk away empty-handed. After selling my house because of him and enduring the mental anguish he caused, I calculated a fair settlement: three hundred thousand dollars plus legal fees.

The ball is now in his court. I've hired my own lawyer, Pepper Bankston—one of the best in the business. With Pepper handling everything, Tony has no reason to contact me directly.

The call comes from a number I don't recognize. I hesitate, debating whether to answer. It could be someone from Meridian with an important update about the meeting. Reluctantly, I swipe to accept the call.

"Hello?" I say cautiously.

"Sienna?"

My steps falter, my heart tightening in my chest. I freeze. "Tony? How did you get this number?"

"Sienna, I need you to do something for me," he says abruptly, skipping any formalities.

I cringe. Of course. That's the first thing he says after everything he's put me through.

"Say you filled out the application to get your YPM band," he continues, barreling on without waiting for my response. "Because we both need to legitimize the readings from our bands, right? Right."

His audacity stuns me. I'm still stuck on, *How did you get my number?* and *What the hell does 'legitimize our readings' even mean?*

Tony doesn't believe in two-way conversations. Just last week, in my session with Ethan, we deconstructed my relationship with my soon-to-be ex-husband. It became glaringly obvious: Tony has very little respect for anyone—not Tanya, not me, and frankly, not even himself.

"Hello," I say again, sharper this time, raising my hand as if he can see me gesturing in exasperation.

"Listen, I don't have a lot of time, which is why I'm talking fast and cutting to the chase," he says, as if entitled to my compliance. "Could you just say we had prior therapy sessions with that guy, Ethan Cranston?"

I shake my head in disbelief, trying to process how utterly wrong this conversation is. To Tony, I must mean as much as a wart on his ass. And by the way, it's Ethan *Clarendon*, not *Cranston*—but I don't bother correcting him.

Then it hits me. I know how he got my number. He

must have hacked into my computer. That's exactly the kind of self-serving, underhanded thing Tony would do to get what he wants. I need to change my passwords. Better yet, I need to figure out how to secure my computer entirely.

But honestly, I'm done. Done with him and his nonsense.

Without another word, I hang up and block his number. I hadn't done it earlier because I didn't think he'd bother calling, especially after the lengths it would take to track down my new number. And now, here he is, asking me to lie about therapy sessions with Ethan? He sounds like he's in real trouble.

Once upon a time, I might've cared enough to wonder what he did to land himself in hot water. But today? I don't give a damn. Frankly, I hope his lies are finally catching up to him. Why would I stop that from happening?

The thought makes me smile. Tony's call hasn't ruined my mood—it's almost improved it. His disturbance hasn't taken the pep out of my stride. I'm still walking on air.

CHAPTER FORTY-EIGHT

TONY

"Damn it," I whisper, glancing around to see if anyone's watching. Nobody is. Still, I can't believe Sienna hung up on me.

Not that it matters. I know she'll come through. When HR calls to confirm what I told them, Sienna will back me up. She always does.

Sure, things have worsened since the last time we saw each other. I should've called her earlier—given us time to talk, to smooth things over, instead of letting our divorce lawyers go to war. That would've been smarter.

But I can't keep leading her on. That's over. She's a good woman, and I don't love her—I can admit that. Still, she's useful. A solid friend when it counts.

I'll make things right, accept the three hundred thousand dollars plus legal fees, and finally, all of this will be over.

But first, I have to deal with what's right in front of me.

I was working at my desk when Andy Bishop's

assistant called. Andy, the President of White Glove Team Technology, usually reaches out directly when he wants to talk. So when I opened an email this morning from "The Desk of Andrew Bishop," it already felt like a bad sign.

He asked me to sit down with Carol Leonhardt in Human Resources to explain, for the record, how my wife and I acquired our YPM bands.

After reading the message, I almost threw up in my trashcan. But I couldn't afford to leave any evidence of how worried I was—or still am.

Carol gave me the impression my explanation was sufficient: Sienna purchased the bands at Innovatech, and we got the go-ahead to wear them and seek our matches from her current, regular therapist, Ethan Cranston. But apparently, there's another hurdle to clear.

Whatever's going on—whatever they think they have on me—I can beat it. I just have to handle things carefully. Besides, I've covered my ass pretty perfectly.

James isn't here. Sure, he could make a lot of accusations if he were, but could he prove any of them? I doubt it.

As I step out of the elevator on the seventeenth floor, I visualize myself standing strong, steering the entire meeting with Andy. I walk confidently through the space, exchanging hellos here and there, winking at one assistant and then another.

I've covered my ass pretty effectively. After my meeting with Carol, I created a receipt from Innovatech and discreetly planted it on Sienna's computer. While I was at it, I also extracted her new phone number from her Messenger. Honestly, I'm still surprised she didn't text me the updated number herself—then again, I probably shouldn't be.

As I step into Andrew's suite, greeted by his grinning assistant—who's unmistakably making eyes at me—I feel a tightening in my gut. She directs me to go right in, and I oblige, adjusting my tie as I walk toward the door.

But the moment I step inside, my chest tightens, and my breath catches. My gaze sweeps over the unexpected faces seated on the furniture.

Sitting on the short sofa, legs crossed and gaze icy, is the one person who's been ghosting me for over a month. And what the hell? In the armchair, her eyes boring into me with a fierce scowl, is Sara.

"Close the door," Andrew says, his voice sharp, his face beet red and twisted into a grimace.

Nobody's smiling. Nobody's even pretending to be pleasant.

And that includes me—because now, it's time to go to war.

CHAPTER FORTY-NINE

TONY

Be *calm.* This is nothing. In the grand scope of things, it's just a minor blip.

I block out Sara and James, even though I could strangle them both if I were alone with them. My focus is solely on Andy, his mouth moving as his words slice through my thoughts with sharp precision. He talks about the value of Quantum Matching Inc. as a client, the trust they've placed in us, and how we're expected to uphold that trust—not exploit the access they've granted.

Then, it starts.

"It's come to my attention—" Andy begins. I sit up straighter, locking eyes with him, my expression steady and composed. "That you acquired your YPM band through unauthorized means," he finishes.

"I can assure you, I have not done what you're claiming," I say, my tone firm and unwavering.

Andy shifts his attention to James. I refuse to look at

him, but I can almost feel him squirming. At least, that's what I expect. *Coward.* All he had to do was check a single box, and we could've avoided this entire mess. But James, in his shortsightedness, has taken it too far. What he doesn't realize is that I covered my ass—not his.

"James, is that true?" Andy asks, his tone sharp.

"No," James replies, his voice unexpectedly steady.

It's enough to catch my attention. I glance at him, expecting the usual timid, red-faced display of guilt. But James isn't shrinking into his seat. He's composed. Confident.

I shrug, feigning indifference. "Whatever. This guy has an ax to grind with me. He quit without notice and wouldn't answer my calls or texts. I thought that was unprofessional of him. I never asked him to do anything beyond the scope of his job," I assert, keeping my tone casual. And that's true—I didn't. Not at first.

Andy narrows his eyes and flips through the document in front of him. "What did you mean," he says slowly, "by texting James, 'Her match submitted a help ticket. Ethan Cranston,' and 'We're not done—checkmark—do it.'"

He looks up, pinning me with a stare that demands an answer.

"Actually, his name is Ethan Clarendon," Sara interjects, her voice slicing through the tension like a blade. "I've met him. I know him."

I lock eyes with her, and instantly, I know—she knows what I've done.

Heat crawls up my neck, prickling my skin, and I

feel it pooling in my face. They're all staring at me, wait-ing. Expecting me to say something. To explain myself. To confess.

THE PAST

NEW YEARS EVE 2098

CHAPTER FIFTY

TONY

E verything is just right—meticulously planned, just the way I like it. I'm finally doing it: getting married before the clock runs out.

Shit, I'm thirty-five. My bride is thirty-one. A good age—not too young, not too old. If things don't work out, she'll still have time to move on. So will I. But things *will* work out.

Reign, my brother, doesn't think so. He's convinced I'll lose interest in her, even if she is, as he put it, "classically beautiful, elegant, and sweet." It's clear he likes Sienna. I have a nagging feeling he wishes he'd met her first. Honestly, I've caught her looking at him in a way that suggests the feeling might be mutual.

He decided to share his opinion during my bachelor party, of all places. Naked asses bouncing around us, tits waving on stage—and what's on his mind? Telling me I'm doomed to screw this up.

"You'll lose interest because you have a problem," he slurred, too drunk to keep his eyes open.

"And what problem is that?" I asked, taking the bait. I was sober—I don't like losing control. That's not my style.

Reign tossed his oversized head back, laughing like an idiot. "Oh no..." He shook his head, grinning smugly. "I'll leave it to you to figure it out. You wouldn't get it even if I broke it down piece by piece and spoon-fed it to you. Then you'd just blame me for trying to mess up your extravagantly orchestrated big day. And I'm not giving you the satisfaction."

What he said was supposed to sting, but I brushed it off. Fuck him. I don't care what Reign thinks of me. He makes a quarter of my salary, and I'm the one with the woman he can't stop obsessing over.

My suit? Declan Ashforth Premium Collection. Custom cut, personally signed by Declan Ashforth himself. And I look damn good in it—check.

Sienna's dress? Specially made by Diamond Diamond. My girl Rebecca got it handmade so my bride can shine next to me. I haven't seen the dress yet, but I've been assured it's nothing short of spectacular. I trust Rebecca, so... check.

The venue? Eterna Tide Pavilion, perched right off the Pacific Coast in Malibu. The same place where Jack Coates married Lemon Asper—two of the most famous A-listers on the planet. The guest list at this venue reads like Hollywood royalty. My wedding committee nailed it. They booked the only venue in the country I found acceptable. Check.

"Hey, Tony. It's 11:30 p.m. Almost showtime," my buddy Jimmy calls, knocking on the door.

I reserved this private room for myself—to reflect before taking the big leap. And I'm not ashamed to call it off if I don't feel it.

Most of my work colleagues, including my boss, are here. All my fraternity brothers showed up. My mother, tasked with ensuring Sienna arrives looking presentable, is here. Even my brother, still bitter he's not my best man, is here. There are people I haven't spoken to in years, invited only because they're successful.

In total: five hundred guests.

If I called it off, I'd tell them all to head straight to the glasshouse on the cliff—the reception area, where we'd party under the stars, surrounded by 180-degree ocean views.

The thing about Sienna is, I could call it off, and she would still want me. Still love me. No matter what, she wants this. But me...

I take a deep breath and try to picture my future with this one woman. My offspring. A new house— maybe in Brentwood, where it's more family-friendly. Sienna would be a great mother: gentle, caring, and so damn kind. Always kind. She's nothing like my mother.

Check.

I turn my head and call over my shoulder, "Here I come, Jim!"

I am going to meet my forever, my future, who will be pronounced my wife at 12:01 a.m. on the dot.

MONDAY, JANUARY 12, 2099

CHAPTER FIFTY-ONE

TONY

I did whatever it took to land the Quantum Match Inc. account—even cutting my honeymoon in Fiji short to have dinner with Karter Reynolds. He's the nephew of Mia McNeily, the quantum physicist who discovered quantum matching and created the YPM band. Karter, a quantum physicist himself, also happens to be the Vice President of Product Development.

Not everyone gets a sit-down with him, but one of my fraternity brothers, who's in Karter's circle, made it happen.

Sienna understood why we couldn't stay for the entirety of our honeymoon. Honestly, it was starting to feel repetitive—what else can you really do on an island besides eat, fuck, and snorkel? By day two, I was already itching to get back into the mix. Regardless, Sienna knows I'm doing this for both of us.

Dinner was held at The Cube, a five-star, glass orb-shaped restaurant designed to look like it's floating along the edge of Sunset Boulevard. Under the orange glow of its ambient lights, I shined. Landing the Quantum Match Inc. account required a delicate dance of reading the room and playing my part to perfection.

For instance, when Karter Reynolds started bragging about how vital he was to the creation of quantum matching technology, I leaned in, feigning curiosity. "Really? Tell me more," I said, though I couldn't have cared less about the origins of the technology. I wasn't being a jerk; I just don't dwell on the past. My focus is always on the future. And in my future, I needed this account.

Karter shared a story about how a single interaction with his aunt, Mia McNeily, sparked the creation of quantum matching technology.

"It all started in the hospital," he began. "She came to visit my grandmother, and after spending time with the adults in the hospital room, she joined me in the waiting room."

He explained that he'd always been in awe of Mia. She didn't visit often, but her reputation as a scientist had left an impression. Wanting to impress her in return, he showed her something he'd learned in his fourth-grade science class.

"Put your hand up, Aunt Mia," he told her.

She obliged, and he placed his smaller palm just shy of hers. "Can you feel that?" he asked her. "That's our energy."

When Karter mentioned the hospital, it jogged my memory. I'd read about that story before—it was a favorite of Mia's on the interview circuit before she retired. She's now living in Monterey, far removed from public life. No amount of money or accolades could bring her back into the spotlight. She's an enigma, but aren't most brilliant minds?

Dinner with Karter was a triumph. I nailed it.

The following week, he and his team met with me, my team, and Andy. We ironed out the details: the features they wanted programmed into the YPM band and upgrades to improve efficiency. I assigned James, my best programmer, to lead the project.

Now, I'm at my desk, staring at ten current models of the YPM band lined up before me. What an intriguing piece of hardware. They look like sleek, solid silver bracelets, but inside, they house a network of rare electromagnetic metals and charged particles activated by the human body. We've been given a diagram of "free zones" within the bands—areas designated for programming the requested features.

I stare so hard at the bands it feels like I'm seeing through them. I'm having a moment of clarity, a solid *what if?*

If I'm honest, I've been asking myself that question for a while now. Not long after I proposed to Sienna, Andy mentioned in a meeting that Quantum Match Inc. was unhappy with their current programming provider and looking for a replacement. I remember the look in Andy's eyes—hungry, determined. He wanted that account.

I glanced around the table at the other Senior Product Integration Team Managers. We were all predators, circling the same prey.

For three days, I made call after call to old connections. Eventually, Amir Maddox, a fellow Omega Psi Phi fraternity brother, got me to the table with Karter Reynolds.

But even then, during those whirlwind days of chasing the account, that question haunted me:

What if?

What if Sienna isn't the one? What if there's someone better—my perfect match?

My perfect match would have to be beautiful— maybe even more stunning than Sienna. Kindness or accommodation? Not necessary. Those traits are already starting to wear on me. I need fire. I *like* fire. Grace? Not so much. My match should be magnificent—someone extraordinary enough to make replacing my wife seem inevitable. I can't quite articulate it, but I'll know her when I see her.

The YPM bands on my desk have recently been acti-vated. They arrived after lunch. Andy approved a mixed team of engineers from various departments to act as product testers, all required to be unmarried.

My fingertips brush across the cool metal of one of the bands. The device is always cold, which is why it's designed with a heating mechanism that gently presses against the skin. Of course, I'm not single. But I *am* the executive leading the team, and they're waiting for me to bring over the bands so they can get started on the project.

Something stirs inside me—curiosity, maybe yearn-ing. I can't say for sure. But without hesitation, I take one of the bands and slip it into my desk drawer.

This one is mine. I can't let anyone see me wearing

it, but still, it's mine. Tomorrow, I'll place an order for ten more. We can have as many test bands and accounts as necessary to get the job done. No one will miss one.

Sharp knocking startles me, yanking me out of my thoughts. I jump slightly and glance toward the door. The blinds are closed because I wanted this moment—my private time with the product—to remain undisturbed. To ensure that, I sent Julie, my assistant, to another product meeting to take notes on my behalf.

I consider asking who it is, but that would make me sound like I'm hiding something. Which, well...

I hop to my feet, adopting the lightest mood possible, and open the door. Standing there is Sara Wilder, a Software Integration Team Leader. She's not in my department, and we've hardly exchanged more than a few pleasantries.

"Hi, Anthony," she says, wiggling her fingers in a playful wave. Her tone is chipper, but her eyes are sharp. It's obvious she's here for something only I can give her, and I already have a pretty good idea of what it is.

"Just call me Tony," I reply, pasting on a polite smile.

"I heard you're supervising the quantum matching project." Her grin grows wider.

"Yes," I reply, my tone curt, cutting to the chase—answering her unspoken question about testing one of the bands before she even asks.

Her eyes widen, and the corners of her mouth stretch into an unstoppable grin. "Are you saying yes... and yes?"

That actually makes me laugh. "Indeed. I'm saying yes..." I stride back to my desk, pick up one of the bands, and return quickly, holding it out to her. "And yes."

But then I stop, pulling the band back just as she reaches for it.

"Wait. Are you married?"

"Nope!" Her enthusiasm is almost comical.

Satisfied, I hand over the band. Happy I've made someone else's day. A small, good deed.

And, yes, I feel a bit absolved.

THURSDAY, MARCH 5, 2099

CHAPTER FIFTY-TWO

TONY

I've been staring out my office window for what feels like hours. My thoughts are a tangled mess, and I can't think straight—let alone get any work done—until I figure out what to do.

I've opened Pandora's box, chasing after something I was never meant to know. I shouldn't know her name—Latanya Peer. I shouldn't have seen her, either. But I did. She's stunning, the kind of beauty that makes your knees weak and sends a rush of blood to places you'd rather not acknowledge in the middle of the workday. Day and night, I'm consumed by thoughts of her. I never believed one look could ignite this kind of... hunger.

If I'm honest, I've never believed in quantum matching. Even when I pursued the account, my focus was on the sixty million in billing—and the five percent cut that came with it. I lumped it in with astrology and other pseudoscience: just another self-fulfilling prophecy dressed up in tech.

But now? Now, I'm experiencing something extraordinary. Something I never expected.

I try to focus on the glow of my computer screen, the data streaming in front of me. I'm logged into Quantum Matching Inc.'s mainframe using master credentials that, for security purposes, only James is supposed to access. I've already broken multiple protocols to get here, and the swirling mix of anguish and desire is eating me alive.

I release a shaky breath, glancing at my fists clenched tight on the desktop. The blinds on my windows are open. Outside, everyone is working diligently in their cubicles, heads down, silent. The main floor is rarely lively. Even so, I hate being stationed here.

I brought Quantum Match Inc. into this company, yet here I am, stuck in this corner while the executives on the fifteenth floor enjoy their private offices. It's something Andy and I need to discuss on Monday—I've worked too hard to settle for anything less.

But for now, I can't afford to linger on petty grievances. Any further steps will push me into truly dangerous territory.

As it stands, I can't reach out to Latanya Peer. My profile isn't in their regular customer database. As far as she knows, her match hasn't engaged with the technology yet.

If I'd done things the right way, the first step would've been purchasing a YPM band from a certified dealer. My personal information would've been uploaded to the system, and the band activated. By now, Latanya would have received the coveted "golden ticket" from Quantum Matching Inc., informing her that her perfect match had been identified.

But I can't create an account the standard way—not without Sienna's consent. I'm married. We're newly-weds. Would she ever agree to this? Of course not.

And yet, Latanya—with her face, her skin, her come-hither smile—she consumes me. My desire for her is uncontrollable, almost like an addiction. No, not almost. This *is* an addiction. A craving that counteracts reason and decency.

Because yes, it is indecent to betray my new wife this way. That much, I acknowledge.

But still…

The battle rages inside me, good and evil clashing like titans. Yet above the chaos, a singular, driven part of me rises, undeterred. My hands move with precision, almost on autopilot. Using James' access, I upload my test user account to Quantum Matching Inc.'s main-frame, bypassing every safeguard.

Soon, Latanya Peer will receive her golden ticket.

CHAPTER FIFTY-THREE

I arrived home late tonight on purpose. Sienna had been calling me all afternoon, asking if I'd be late for dinner. I didn't have the heart to blow her off outright. She's been excited about the meal she's prepared—Chilean sea bass dumplings with snow peas and carrots on a bed of jasmine rice. She even boasted about it on the phone.

"All the flavors are there, Tony. It's authentic Asian cuisine."

Sweet, beautiful Sienna, always eager to please me—which I like. How will I ever tell her what I've done?

Not even half an hour after my profile went live, Latanya Peer—Tanya—accepted entering the quantum match process with me. Together, we've flown through the steps at warp speed. We're already at the first meeting stage. Tanya practically pleaded that we meet tonight for drinks, but I still have a wife. And that wife has made dinner for us.

To honor her, I put off meeting Tanya until

tomorrow for lunch in Manhattan Beach—far enough away to avoid running into anyone I know. Tanya's picture has stirred something unexpected within me, but will I feel the same when I meet her in real life? I don't know.

For all I know, this technology could still be a sham. I've always loved a pretty face like Tanya's—with or without quantum matching. But tomorrow, I'll find out for sure. Tonight, though? Happy wife, happy life.

Still, something nags at me, holding me back from fully diving in. I'm more than capable of telling Sienna to pack up dinner, put it on ice, and not wait up. But I haven't—because Tanya isn't a permanent match. Not really. I manipulated the system to say she is.

I made the change out of caution, worried Tanya would see we're only a temporary match and decide to pass on meeting me altogether. According to QM Inc.'s data, people often wait for lifetime matches, unwilling to waste time on reasons or seasons. And as much as I hate to admit it, I get it.

So for now, Sienna is still my priority.

That might change tomorrow.

I leave my car, walk through the garage, and enter the house. It's time to be a good husband.

"Sienna, I'm home!" I call.

"I'm in the kitchen," she replies.

And now it's time to play our roles.

SUNDAY, JUNE 3, 2099

CHAPTER FIFTY-FOUR

TONY

I sit alone in my car, parked in the garage. The engine is off, but my thoughts roar like an untamed beast. I've rehearsed this moment so many times I could recite it like a script. I've got this. It should be easy. I *should* feel guilt—but I don't.

My relationship with Tanya has been too good, too consuming to leave space for regret. There's no denying it—I am a cheater. I've explored Tanya's body like a traveler discovering uncharted terrain, savoring every curve and sensation. Our lovemaking is unparalleled. When we connect, we melt together, becoming one—and pulling apart feels unbearable. I crave her constantly, the memory of her touch haunting my skin even now, as I grip the steering wheel like it's my only tether to reality.

I've thought long and hard about the next steps. When you've found something this miraculous, you'll do whatever it takes to hold onto it. That's why I press the button to open my glove compartment. Inside, two jewelry boxes containing YPM bands rest in wait. The sight of them steadies me. It's time to cover my ass.

Initially, I planned to simply leave Sienna—tell her I'm not in love with her anymore and move on smoothly to Tanya. Because, frankly, I'm not in love with Sienna anymore. I was, once, before I gazed into Tanya's magnetic eyes and felt the softness of her lips against mine.

Now, it's impossible to imagine a future without Tanya. She's the object I unleashed from Pandora's box, and I feel destined to chase her until my last breath.

But things have become more complicated. James knows what I've done.

The night it all came to light, I was in my office late, having lost track of time while on the phone with Tanya. She knows I'm married—though I told her Sienna is aware of my match and is waiting to meet her own. That lie, which I *do* regret, has eased Tanya's conscience. She carries no guilt in continuing this affair with me.

Then I heard something outside my office door. A faint noise, enough to make me pause mid-sentence. I told Tanya I had to go and promised to call her as soon as I was settled in my car.

When I stepped out into the hallway, James was pacing in front of my office door, his movements jittery and uncoordinated, like he was wrestling with something too heavy to hold.

"What are you doing?" I asked, frowning. It was strange behavior, even for him.

He looked wrecked—dark circles under his eyes,

eyelids heavy, as if carrying the burdens of the world on his shoulders. For a moment, I thought it might be something personal. Maybe his girlfriend had dumped him or he'd had a family emergency.

But his answer came in a rush, like it had been building inside him all night.

"I know what you did," he said, his voice shaky and desperate.

"What?" I replied, genuinely confused.

He locked eyes with me, the weight of his words crushing the space between us.

"I know what you did in the Quantum Match mainframe."

I froze. My mind raced through every possible way to shut him up. James is scrawny, timid, and unemotional. One hard hit to the jaw, and he'd probably crumble. But the thought was too dark, even for me. And there are cameras everywhere. The idea of spending my life in jail churned my stomach.

So, I leaned into my strengths: convincing weaker minds to see things my way.

James isn't dangerous. He's jittery, scared that my actions will implicate him—which they will. Technically, my hands are clean. That's why he was unraveling, pacing outside my door like a man who knew his life depended on keeping calm but couldn't quite manage it.

I assured him we'd both be fine if he just worked with me to keep everything smooth and copacetic.

Meeting his frantic gaze, I softened my tone, reached out, and touched his shoulder. "I apologize for overstepping," I said. "In the future, I won't access the main-frame without your permission."

His eyes flickered across my face, searching for any crack in my composure, any sign of insincerity. But I held firm, steady. Eventually, he gave a slow, reluctant nod. "Okay."

I wish I could keep my word.

Yesterday, I purchased two YPM bands and registered their serial numbers under my name and Sienna's. Using James's credentials, I seamlessly transferred data from my test YPM band to the new one. I couldn't have done it without accessing the mainframe as him.

Tonight, I'll lean into my strengths again—this time to sway Sienna into wearing her band. Soon, she'll have her results. I don't know what kind of match the system will turn up for her, but I'm not certain I'm ready to let her go yet.

Will the addiction to Tanya fade when our quantum match ends? Will my love for Sienna return? Maybe that's the plan. Maybe, after I overindulge in Tanya, Sienna will, in the end and forever, be my perfect match.

MONDAY, JULY 20, 2099

CHAPTER FIFTY-FIVE

TONY

Today is a very important day.

Everyone who participated in the quantum matching testing within our company will learn if they've found their perfect match. For those without one, their profiles will go live for free, giving them the opportunity to discover a future connection.

I've timed Sienna's YPM results to align with this day. If her match doesn't mark me as her final destination, I'll need to make some adjustments to her profile.

James, however, hasn't made this process easy. He's operated with a surprising level of tactical finesse—something I didn't think he had in him. He's managed to restrict my ability to use his credentials to access the Quantum Match mainframe. Now, any updates or changes require his fingerprint.

At this juncture, I can't even demand that he remove the restriction. With his newfound backbone, James called an "important" meeting with Andy, himself, and me immediately after implementing the change. He pitched the new security protocol before I even had the chance to corner him.

"It's an extra layer of protection," he explained, his gaze fixed solely on Andy. "Quantum Match Inc. holds incredibly sensitive data. Toby Sullivan, one of their execs, specifically requested we implement this safeguard. He also wants daily access logs."

I knew James was lying. But Andy? He was already nodding, eating up every word like gospel.

Still, I couldn't let it slide. "Daily?" I asked, scoffing as if the suggestion were completely ridiculous. "We can't do that."

"Yes, we can," James replied, his tone flat and emotionless. He still refused to look at me. "I've already started. As of today."

"No. I like it," Andy said briskly, already signaling that he was ready to move on. The man has little patience for unscheduled meetings, and I still don't know what James said to get him to agree to this one. Whatever it was, it worked.

Since then, James and I have been locked in a silent game of chess. But James? He's just a pawn. Sure, he got his fingerprint access protocol approved, but he's sitting at my desk now, and I intend to finish this game.

My office door is locked—privacy is key. I can't risk anyone barging in and disrupting what needs to be done.

"I'll need access to the mainframe," I say, cutting straight to the point.

For the first time in a while, James looks me in the

eye. His expression is a mix of fear and defiance. I can almost feel the turmoil inside him—his stomach twisting into knots, his thoughts weighed down and sluggish.

"What do you need to do?" he finally asks, his voice barely steady.

I lean back in my chair, crossing my arms. "Minor adjustments."

"But no more adjustments need to be made. We've finished—"

I cut him off with a sharp snort. "James. Stop fucking around. Sienna Holloway. I need access to her profile five minutes ago."

His face turns crimson, his hands trembling as he shakes his head. I can see him resisting me, every fiber of his being screaming no. I don't want him this scared. I don't enjoy putting him through this, but unfortunately for him, I need this.

"James, listen," I say, softening my tone. "I know I've made some mistakes. I just need to fix one last thing so that you and I can... you know. Move on."

His brows furrow, and he glances at the locked door, as though considering an escape.

I check my watch. Less than fifteen minutes remain before the meeting with the team and testers. My patience is officially gone.

"Just open the mainframe," I order, my voice hardening.

James throws up his hands, his expression equal parts frustration and fear. "I don't want anything to do with this."

"Fine." I lean forward, making sure he can't look

away. "Open the mainframe, I'll make the adjustments, close it, and you can hand your access back over to Toby."

James hesitates, his hand hovering over the keyboard. The tension stretches unbearably until, finally, he logs in, using a special code to disable the fingerprint access.

My heart lurches as the system unlocks, and a surge of adrenaline courses through me. I can finally do what I've been itching to do.

"Thanks," I mutter, my focus already shifting to the screen.

James steps toward the door, fumbling with the lock. "Will that be all?"

"Yeah," I manage to say, though the word feels caught in my throat.

As soon as I'm alone, my eyes land on Sienna's profile. My pulse quickens, and a tightness grips my chest, like a weight pressing down. Instinctively, I rub at it, trying to ease the discomfort.

No. Way.

The words thunder through my mind as I stare at the screen, refusing to believe what I'm seeing.

This can't stand. I can't let it stand.

I have to fix this.

BACK TO THE PRESENT

TUESDAY, DECEMBER 29, 2099

CHAPTER FIFTY-SIX

"The funniest thing happened to me yesterday," I tell Ethan, leaning back on the plush couch. I feel lighter than I have in months.

"Is that so?" he says, his voice warm and inviting, encouraging me to elaborate.

This is my last therapy session of the year, and as I arrange my thoughts, I marvel at how far I've come. That first afternoon, I'd been a mess—distraught, weighed down by the despair of loving Tony. It's odd how perspective has dulled my appetite for him, how clarity has stripped the shine off what I once thought was the pinnacle of love and partnership. And it's exactly why I have this story to share with Ethan.

"You know I've been hiking in Runyon Canyon every morning," I begin. "For physical fitness, mental acuity—all that good stuff."

"Yes, you mentioned that a few weeks ago."

"Every morning, seven a.m.," I add, proud of my

consistency. This new routine feels like a declaration of independence, a testament to the fact that I'm no longer bogged down by the urge to reclaim what I lost with Tony.

Ethan nods, his expression encouraging, and I continue.

"So, yesterday, I ran into one of Tony's former colleagues on the trail. Her name is Sara..." I pause, snapping my fingers as I try to recall her last name. "Goodness, I don't think I ever got it."

"We don't need her last name, do we?" Ethan quips, his tone light and joking. He has this effortless wit that always puts me at ease. Whoever his match is, she's lucky.

"No," I reply, a smile creeping across my face. Then, out of nowhere, the name surfaces. "Wilder! Her name is Sara Wilder."

Ethan smiles warmly. "Okay. Sara Wilder."

"Yeah... I've always liked her. We could've been really good friends from the start. I remember thinking that the first time we met." My gaze softens as I recall our interaction at last year's Christmas party. "Anyway, we talked like we were old friends—about how I've been, that I'm seeing you. But then I felt a boundary go up because, well, she was Tony's colleague."

Ethan nods slightly, prompting me to go on.

"But she's not his colleague anymore," I add, sitting up straighter. "She told me Tony's employment was terminated for misconduct."

I let out a withering sigh, picturing how Tony must be handling that. *Not well*, I imagine.

"How does that make you feel?" Ethan asks.

I raise my eyebrows thoughtfully. "At first, I wanted to call him, to make sure he was okay. But then I stopped myself and asked, 'Why? What would be the point?' If Tony was fired, he probably did something to deserve it. He is manipulative. And then, another feeling came over me."

A smile spreads across my face, and I sit with it, letting it warm me from the inside out. "Relief. Because now, I'm free to truly be friends with Sara."

"And?" Ethan prods gently, sensing there's more.

"She invited me to a New Year's Eve soiree!" I laugh a little. "That's exactly what she called it—a *soiree*. It's on a yacht."

"And what did you say?"

"I said okay. I mean, I have no other plans. Lena and Leo are off to Manhattan to watch the Apple spark over the city and rain candy for the rats."

Ethan chuckles along with me. The moment feels light, almost celebratory.

"That's good to hear you've made a plan to spend New Year's with a new friend," he says, his tone encouraging.

I press my lips together, hesitating as the uncomfortable part of Sara's invitation lingers in my mind. "The party is being thrown by Sara's perfect match. I mean, everywhere I look, there's a perfect match." My voice edges with frustration, and I realize how much it sounds like I'm complaining—because I am.

Ethan's smile fades just slightly, his tone growing

more measured. "So," he begins, "are you ready to follow up on the Your Perfect Match help ticket?"

"No," I say quickly, almost cutting him off.

His eyes widen slightly, caught off guard by my swift, decisive response. We've worked on avoiding this in our sessions—rushing to answer without giving myself time to process. I'm supposed to pause, reflect, and let my thoughts settle before reaching a carefully considered conclusion.

Ethan leans back in his chair, his expression softening into curiosity. He doesn't push, giving me the space to explain.

"I mean, not yet," I add, my tone softening. "Maybe next year. The work I'm doing with Meridian takes up so much of my time, and it's fulfilling. Who knows? Maybe I'll meet someone there the old-fashioned way." I scrunch my nose, instantly regretting the comment. "Not that I'm against the technology," I say hastily. "It's just… after everything I've been through, I need a break from it for a while."

Ethan nods slowly, letting my words settle. "Well," he says after a moment of thought, "I think you and I have gone as far as we needed to go."

My eyebrows knit together in confusion. "What?" I squeak.

Ethan's smile is calm, reassuring—the kind of expression he uses when delivering something important but kind. "How about we go back to being friends, Sienna? Starting…" He glances at his watch, and instinctively, I do the same. Only then do I realize how much time has passed—our session has gone well over the hour.

I let out a small laugh, a mix of nervousness and relief. "Good thing I'm not paying for this, or I'd be in serious debt by now," I mutter under my breath.

"Now," Ethan says with finality, his tone warm but resolute.

We smile at each other, testing the waters of this new relationship—though, really, it feels like we're picking up where we left off during that first dinner.

"And so, Sienna," Ethan begins, his tone steady and warm. "As your friend, I really want you to promise me one thing: don't ever close yourself off to love. Could you do that for me?"

My tongue freezes against the back of my teeth as I pause, struck by the sincerity in his eyes. It's disarming—this genuine care for my happiness. And then it hits me: I've never known someone who truly cared about my well-being like this.

Well, that's not entirely true. Lena and Leo care. And the more I get to know Sara, I suspect she will too. It dawns on me that I'm rebuilding something I've never fully had—a solid tribe of people to love and be loved by, unconditionally.

"Don't worry if you choose never to be ready," Ethan says, mistaking the tears that are now streaming down my cheeks. His voice holds the same calm reassurance I've come to depend on, even as he misreads the moment. Which surprises me—how could he not know?

"No," I murmur, my voice trembling as he hands me

the box of tissues. "No, that's not it." I nod, giving myself a moment to gather the words, and begin again. "I won't close myself off to love." My voice steadies, my heart swelling with gratitude. "And thank you... thank you for caring."

THURSDAY, DECEMBER 31, 2099

CHAPTER FIFTY-SEVEN

It's 9:30 PM. Why do I have butterflies fluttering in my stomach tonight? Maybe it's because exactly one year ago, on this very date, I was the most nervous I had ever been. It still feels surreal that I planned and had an entire wedding ceremony—only for it to crumble so quickly afterward.

I chuckle softly to myself. Sometimes, when I replay those memories, it feels so tragically absurd that all I can do is laugh—a kind of laugh that carries the weight of acceptance.

Sara called me earlier to make sure I hadn't changed my mind about attending tonight. She sounded positively elated.

"I can't wait for you to meet him," she gushed about her match. "He is one of the greatest human beings you'll ever meet. Everybody loves him, and you will too."

Sara's enthusiasm for her perfect match is contagious. She truly adores him, and honestly? I find it kind of adorable—and inspiring. After that conversation, I couldn't help but wonder if I've been too hasty in shutting the door to new possibilities.

And so… here I am.

Tonight, I've been meticulous about how I look. My sex hormones feel like they've reignited, sparking back to life in full force. Who knows who I'll meet at this New Year's Eve soiree? I even treated myself to a little shopping spree yesterday for a brand-new outfit.

It's a monumental New Year's celebration, after all —the dawn of a new century, the 2100s. Unless I live to be a hundred and thirty-two years old, I won't be around to celebrate the dawn of 2200. That's another reason why I plan to make the most of tonight!

I settled on a silver slinky silk spaghetti-strap dress that flows elegantly with my every step. To shield myself from the chill, I paired it with a full-length silver faux fur coat, soft and luxurious against my skin. My hair is coiled high in an intricate, elegant bun that gleams in the light. For the first time in forever, I'm wearing eyeshadow—a soft shimmer that catches the glow of the evening. I went all out tonight, and it feels good. Liberating, even.

As I glance around the bustling Swift train, packed with other New Year's Eve revelers, I don't mind the crowd. The energy is palpable, electrifying. My stop is coming up soon—the San Pedro Pier. My coat will keep me warm as I step off into the crisp night air, ready to embrace whatever this evening has in store.

The sleek, automated voice announces my arrival. As I step off the Swift, the cool night air wraps around me, refreshing and invigorating. The crowd swells around me, buzzing with the excitement of New Year's Eve. I tilt my head back to take in the stars—clear, bright, and scattered across the sky like confetti. For a moment, the night feels full of promise, as though anything might happen.

Pulling my phone from my coat pocket, I open the instructions Sara sent—five detailed reminders, complete with screenshots and diagrams. She's nothing if not thorough. Her directions are easy to follow, and soon I'm swept along with the flow of elegantly dressed partygoers heading toward the pier.

Then, I see it.

The "vessel" Sara mentioned isn't just a yacht—it's massive, more like a small cruise ship. Its sleek white exterior gleams under the dock's floodlights, and dazzling strings of lights decorate its decks. A sense of awe hits me. This is the life Sara's perfect match lives in? Did she say he owned it? She did. *Wow.*

The line moves quickly as people, dressed in glittering gowns and sharp suits, ascend the ramp with ease. I join the queue, pulling up the electronic boarding pass Sara sent me.

I'm about to scan it when a voice cuts through the hum of the crowd.

"What's she doing here?"

The words are low but pointed, spoken by a woman just to my right.

There are plenty of "shes" in this crowd, but something in her tone—the deliberate pause, the sharp edge —tells me it's directed at me.

I glance over and freeze.

CHAPTER FIFTY-EIGHT

O ff to the side, standing with two men in crisp black suits, are Tanya and Tony. My stomach flips, a cold shock slicing through the warm excitement of the night. Tanya's gaze is locked on me, her expression a mix of frustration and outright anger. Tony's face—stoic yet undeniably tense —catches the glow of the ship's lights.

What are they doing here? Given how Sara feels about Tony, it doesn't make sense. The way she spoke about him made me think he was a pariah to her— someone she wanted nothing to do with.

"Sorry, sir, ma'am, you're not on the list," one of the suited men says firmly.

"Tony, do something!" Tanya snaps, her voice rising as she glances around frantically.

But Tony doesn't move. He's still staring at me, his gaze distant, unreadable. The tension in his face is unmistakable, but his eyes—there's something strange about them, almost lost.

"What are you looking at *her* for?" Tanya shrieks, completely unraveling as she follows his line of sight to me.

I hadn't realized just how jarring it is to see them both until I feel my hand pressing against my chest, trying to calm my racing heart.

I shake my head and turn away, refusing to let them ruin my night. I take slow, measured breaths, reminding myself that every step I take in the present carries me further into the future, while the past becomes distant, walled off. That's how I think about Tony these days—barricaded behind the wall of my past.

The line moves forward, and soon, I'm inside. As the tempered glass doors close behind me, I'm greeted by warmth and light. The space is alive—vibrant and buzzing with energy. Strings of fairy lights cast a golden glow over the scene, which feels like it's straight out of a dream.

There's a full jazz band playing a lively tune, tables laden with food that looks too beautiful to eat, and a bar stretching along the far wall. Waitstaff weave seamlessly through the crowd, offering drinks and hors d'oeuvres to anyone too engrossed in conversation to make their way to the tables. Laughter bubbles everywhere, and for the first time in what feels like forever, I feel genuinely excited. *This* is how the new me starts the new century!

Determined not to let the night slip by unnoticed, I glance around, scanning the crowd. I will not be wallpaper tonight. My resolution is firm. I'm here to socialize, to laugh, to embrace this new chapter of my life.

Then, near the band, I see her—Sara. She's talking animatedly with a waiter, her smile radiant.

"Sara!" I call, my voice cutting through the music.

"Sienna!" she exclaims at the same time, her face lighting up when she spots me.

We rush toward each other, meeting in a warm hug. It feels like we're old friends, even though we've barely scratched the surface of knowing each other. The moment is joyful and effortless—an anchor in the chaos of my evening.

But then, just as I'm pulling back, a familiar figure steps out of the crowd, wrapping his arms around Sara from behind. She leans into him, beaming, and to my shock, they kiss. It's the kind of kiss that screams, *This is my person.*

My breath catches as my brain struggles to reconcile what I'm seeing.

What...?

And then it hits me like a lightning bolt.

CHAPTER FIFTY-NINE

"Is he...?" I whisper, my voice hoarse with emotion as I stare at Sara and—
Ethan.

Is he her match? Because they look unmistakably YPM with their arms wrapped around each other, holding on like their love is the only thing tethering them to the earth.

I'm stunned, running on autopilot as I step forward to hug him too. "You own this boat, Ethan?" I ask, disbelief flooding my voice.

Sara takes my hands firmly in hers, her gaze locking with mine. "Breathe, Sienna," she says gently.

I hadn't realized how shallow my breaths had become until I try for a deep inhale. By the third one, my head stops spinning so much.

"Let's get her somewhere private," Ethan says. He leaves Sara's side to stand on my other, guiding me with a supportive arm around my waist.

I can't believe I'm actually walking. A million questions whirl in my mind—*When? How did they find out they were each other's match? Should I be angry? Should I feel betrayed?* I don't know yet.

Sara moves through the vessel with a familiarity that suggests she's been here many times before. Ethan follows, steady and composed. So, I guess Ethan is rich enough to own a boat like this.

They lead me to a private parlor, a stunning space outfitted with white plush sectionals and sleek silver tables.

We sit close together, even though the couches could easily accommodate fifty people or more.

"How are you feeling, Sienna?" Ethan asks in his familiar, calm tone. "Other than confused."

I narrow my eyes at him, ignoring the question entirely. "Do you own this boat?" I ask again, my voice sharper this time.

"I wish," he says, a small smile tugging at his lips. "This vessel belongs to Alexander Creston."

My jaw drops, and for a moment, words fail me. There's too much to process. *Alexander Creston?* Of course I know who he is. You can't work in environmental law and not know his name.

"He's a philanthropist and an—" Sara begins.

"I know who and what he is," I interrupt, my voice barely audible. Breathless.

I catch the way Sara takes a deep, steadying breath, and the look she and Ethan exchange—a glance so loaded with meaning it's like an unspoken conversation.

"Sienna," Sara says carefully. "I'm going to drop something heavy on you, something that will explain why we're here together and why Ethan didn't tell you about me. But I need you to listen—really listen—until I finish explaining. Are you okay with that?"

After a deep inhale and an equally long exhale, I nod.

Sara begins to unravel the story. She explains that she asked Tony to let her participate in the quantum matching project as a tester. Tony agreed, but she soon discovered he broke protocol and wore his own YPM band.

Earlier this month, Sara and James—whom I'd heard Tony mention often—confronted him in Andrew Bishop's office. They pressured him until he admitted he had manipulated the system, switching his match with Tanya from temporary to permanent.

"That's why we believe he was leading you on," Sara says, her voice thick with anger. "He wanted to keep you on ice for when things with Tanya inevitably fizzled out."

My chest tightens as the pieces fall into place, each revelation cutting deeper. But Sara isn't finished.

"And then he did something even worse," she says, her voice trembling. "He tampered with your match, Sienna—your permanent match."

The words hit me like a freight train. *My permanent match.*

I glance instinctively at Ethan.

"And so, Anthony decided to play with my future, my happiness too," Sara continues, her voice breaking slightly. She clings to Ethan's arm, so close she might as well be sitting on his lap. It doesn't feel wrong—it feels right. They look… perfect together.

"But you said your match owns the boat," I say, the words tumbling out before I can stop them. It's all I can manage as my mind races, grasping for clarity.

Sara's lips curve into a small, knowing smile. "Well," she says softly, "I consider Alexander my match-match. He'll always be a dear friend to me." She pauses, her smile widening as she glances at Ethan and leans into him. "But this one here? He's my *perfect* match."

"Sienna?" Ethan asks gently, his voice snapping me out of my spiraling thoughts.

I sit up instinctively, as though trained to respond. "Yes," I reply automatically.

He's about to speak when someone new enters the room—a commanding presence that immediately shifts the energy.

We've just been joined by the owner of the vessel.

CHAPTER SIXTY

I t is true.
   It is so…
   Very…
Very…
Very…
True.

The moment my eyes meet Alexander Creston's, something inexplicable happens—something beyond words. I feel a part of myself, something spiritual, rising from my body to meet him in the air above us. It's as if I am floating through the cosmos, weightless, as I rise to my feet.

"Hi," I whisper, barely able to press the word out of my throat.

"Hi," he replies, his voice a soft echo of my own.

Alexander Creston is a beautiful man—so achingly beautiful that he doesn't even seem real. His presence feels otherworldly, as though he stepped out of a dream I never knew I had. Perhaps it's the quantum connection between us, casting him in this cosmic light, making him appear so impossibly perfect. But I can't question it. Not now. Not when I'm so utterly convinced of the truth.

The energy that binds us is undeniable, intelligent, and uniquely human. Its Maker whispers that Alex and I were meant to be.

My knees threaten to buckle as he extends his hand toward me. When I take it, our first touch, it feels as though eternity stretches out before us. In that instant, I see it all—every radiant moment of our forever.

I see our future dates, filled with laughter and shared secrets. I see us lying awake in bed, talking endlessly about everything under the moon, and the sun, and then the moon again, never tiring of each other's voices. We make plans—not just plans to live, but plans to serve a greater purpose, to give back, to leave the world better than we found it.

We have fun wherever we go. We laugh. I never have to guard my words or hide my feelings. With Alex, I am wholly myself—unfiltered, unburdened, unafraid. He accepts me completely, just as I am.

I see a new path unfolding for me. My life changes direction in ways I never imagined. I no longer lecture; instead, I follow a calling I didn't know was waiting for me.

We have children—three of them. Our oldest, a boy, is named Gus. Our daughters are Lima and Maxi. Together, we pour our love into them. We raise them with laughter, wisdom, and warmth. We love them to the moon and back. We love each other to the moon and back.

Our lives are full. Our bond is unshakable. We grow old together, living well into our nineties. We are the picture of a life well lived, a love well nurtured.

When the end comes, Alex goes first. The grief is unbearable, and without him, my heart can't carry on. Just a week later, I follow him into the great unknown.

At our joint funeral, our children—wise, kind, and strong—stand together. They speak with reverence and love, their voices steady with truth.

"And our parents," they say, "lived happily ever after."

Yes, it all comes to me clearly—it's more than wishful thinking—it's set in stone.

SATURDAY, JULY 1, 2102

CHAPTER SIXTY-ONE

TONY

The gates to Sienna and Alex's Montecito estate glide open with effortless grace, welcoming me in a way that feels both cool and grand. I snort, laughing at the irony of it all.

This is my sixth time making the hour-and-a-half drive from LA to their seventy-acre sanctuary—a sprawling expanse primarily used for cultivating crops that have no business thriving in this region. Once, I would've mocked the impracticality of it. Now, I find myself holding a begrudging respect for a man and a woman who have dedicated themselves to something greater than personal gain, operating as true agents of the "greater good."

With a resigned sigh, I roll my windows all the way down, letting the air in—thick with the scent of things growing, sweet and woodsy, carried by the tepid, moisture-laden breeze from the nearby Pacific. It wraps around me, warm and comforting.

Another aspect missing now—one that was alive on

my first visit—is the deep, gnawing sense of dread. Back then, I wasn't honest with anyone, least of all myself. I started this new century by losing everything: my job, my friends, and, of course, Tanya—the woman who vanished from my life the night of Alexander's New Year's Eve Cruise Extravaganza, leaving me high and dry.

Admittedly, that night had been humiliating for both of us. I never told Tanya we had been disinvited, convinced I could handle Sara when we arrived. I always believed Sara to be soft. My plan was simple: show up, flash my winning smile, apologize profusely, admit my faults, and—if necessary—drop to my knees and beg for Tanya to be allowed into the party she had been looking forward to for months.

But then I saw Sienna walking up the ramp.

I froze, as if watching a slow-motion car crash, knowing the impact was inevitable.

Back in Andy's office, when Sara and James had cornered me, Sara claimed she had met Ethan. But then she quickly corrected herself—no, not in person, but they had spoken over the phone. I had felt a brief wave of relief then. The quantum energy effect, the supposed force that bonds perfect matches, could only be triggered through real-life interaction. It didn't matter, though. They still tore me apart in that meeting.

Andy—who had been more than just my boss but a true friend—had no choice but to side against me. The evidence was overwhelming. I had flouted protocol, manipulated the system, and harassed James, abusing my authority to force him into breaking company policy and the law. My firing was inevitable.

Still, I thought I had one last card to play—one last flicker of hope.

Because as I was leaving the office, Sara whispered in disgust, "Frankly, I don't want anything else to do with YPM."

That meant she wouldn't be seeking out her match anytime soon.

So, that's why I was so blindsided when I saw Sienna at the New Year's Eve party.

In that moment, it all clicked—Sara had played me. She hadn't wanted me to know that my carefully crafted house of cards had already been blown away before I even walked into Andy's office. She let me believe I still had control, still had a chance, when in reality, I was already undone.

And so, right there on the pier, I forced myself to do what I had been avoiding all night—I told Tanya the truth.

"We weren't invited," I admitted, my voice barely above the chatter of the crowd boarding the yacht. "I lost my job." I hesitated, but there was no point in stalling. "And... Alexander Creston is Sienna's real perfect match."

Her mouth dropped open, cutting off the demand that had been forming on her lips. Instead of shouting, *Do something, Tony!* she asked, "What are you talking about?"

I couldn't tell her everything. I knew that if I did, I'd lose her completely. And if I was losing her, I needed to at least salvage some respect—what little remained. So, I lied.

"When we were testing upgrades to the YPM Band, I accidentally mixed up the results and assigned Sara Sienna's match," I said, keeping my voice steady, praying she'd buy it.

But Tanya wasn't stupid.

The cold look in her eyes sent a chill down my spine. Her head tilted slightly, her gaze narrowing into slits as she stared at me as if genuinely seeing me for the first time.

She didn't believe a single word I had just said.

And that's when I knew—she was done deluding herself about me. The only thing that could have saved us at that moment was if I could somehow get her inside that party. But I couldn't. And we both knew it.

"You're a horrible person, Tony," she said, her voice eerily composed. Then, with a final, searing blow, she added, "And by the way, I know you fucked Alice. Don't ever call me again."

She walked away, poised, dignified, already erasing me from her life.

And I didn't call after her.

I didn't fight for her.

Because, deep down, I knew—I had nothing left to give.

She had drained me. Squeezed me dry. And now, I was empty.

I SPENT WEEKS CHASING MY TAIL, DOING EVERYTHING I could to reclaim my dignity.

Word spread quickly—everyone in my industry knew I had been fired. No one knew exactly why, though. As part of my forced resignation, I agreed to keep the details sealed, ensuring my misconduct wouldn't scare off future clients or damage the company's relationship with Quantum Matching Inc.

But it didn't matter.

People *knew*.

They didn't need specifics to recognize that I had done something very wrong. And that was enough to make me unhirable.

Sure, they paid me well to walk away—enough to strike out on my own. But that wasn't good enough for me back then.

I needed my status back.

I missed walking into work and feeling important—being someone people had to respect. I missed the executive meetings, the competition, the constant climb up the ranks. If they had given me just three more years, I would have had the job I was gunning for.

I would have had Andy's job.

And I would have plotted, planned, and stabbed him in the back to get it.

Because that was who I was.

That was the person I used to be.

And if someone were to ask me now, How did you change?

Well… that's a story worth telling.

CHAPTER SIXTY-TWO

TONY

My transformation began with yet another scheme I had cooked up.

I wasn't wrong about Sara—she *was* forgiving. And she knew the right people, the kind who could put me back in the lineup. One call from her to the right colleague, and I'd be back on track to heading a major corporation.

So, I called her.

I laid it on thick—apologies dripping with remorse, my voice heavy with regret.

"You should see someone," she said.

"See someone? What do you mean by *see* someone?" I asked, though I already knew. I just hoped she wouldn't suggest *him*.

Sara and her match—her husband now—had eloped in Vegas on the first Monday of the New Year. I had no interest in sitting across from her new *perfect* man, letting him dissect me like I was some kind of lost cause.

"I'll ask Ethan to recommend a therapist for you," she said.

Then, in her usual no-nonsense way, she added, "And don't screw around with my time, Anthony. I want you to actually see this person. That's the only way I could ever fully trust you."

And that was it.

She didn't even have to say it outright—I knew it was the only way she'd ever vouch for me again.

When Ethan called, I was prepared for a stiff, clinical professional, detached and impersonal. Instead, he pitched himself as my therapist.

He said he relished difficult projects. And I was just that.

During our first session, Ethan saw right through me. He knew I was screwing around, being manipulative, playing a game. But he worked on me anyway, chipping away at the facade I was trying so hard to maintain.

I have to admit—I liked it. The game of cat and mouse. The way he unearthed truths I had buried deep within myself, forcing me to lay them out on the table, raw and undeniable.

Yes, I was just as selfish as Tanya.

Yes, my mother was self-centered, which meant I had to become just as self-regarding in order to survive.

That was my first real breakthrough. That was when I wept for real.

Every week, I saw him—four times a month.

Then, one day, he suggested I call Sienna and Alex. He told me to apologize for what I had done.

That was the moment I felt truly at a crossroads.

Ethan was giving me exactly what I had been seeking—redemption, or at least the appearance of it. If I called and apologized to Sienna, Sara would hear about it. And if Sara believed in my transformation, maybe she'd vouch for me. Maybe she'd mention my name to the right people—the ones looking for a seasoned Lead Programmer.

She had recently been named Chief Technology Officer at White Glove Team Technology. The job *I* wanted.

No… I was not happy.

Yes… I was bitter.

But I hid it well.

What could I do about it, anyway? She had won. I had lost.

Acceptance.

That's how I tolerated her success. That's how I convinced myself to move forward.

And so, I called Sienna. Following Ethan's instructions, I asked if we could meet in person. I braced myself for her to tell me to go to hell—after all, I had tried to snatch her happily ever after away from her. But no. She sounded cheery when she said, "Of course, Tony. But I'm in Montecito right now. Could you drive out?"

I wanted to say no. I wanted to suggest something more convenient for *me*. But instead, I said I would.

During the drive, a deep resentment churned inside me. Look at what Sienna is making me do. First Sara, now her. These women had me by the balls, and they were squeezing—hard.

I knew that was the wrong attitude. Ethan and I had talked about my relationship with emasculation and how I let the mere perception of losing control send me into a spiral. I thought about that. I thought about something else he had said, too—that he knew I still had an agenda. Because despite all the progress I had made, I had not yet hit rock bottom.

And then, when I arrived, there it was—creamy sausage tortellini with freshly made focaccia—my favorite.

If Alexander hadn't joined us, I might have thought Sienna was trying to make amends, to show me she still loved me, that maybe she preferred me over him.

But I vanquished that thought as soon as it surfaced. Ethan had warned me—giving and receiving isn't always transactional, especially not with Sienna. You never really knew your ex-wife at all, he had said.

Yet by the time I sat down on the open-air patio, the resentment had returned, gnawing at my insides. The view stretched out before me—perfectly aligned glass greenhouses cultivating coffee from regions all over the world. The life she had built here. It had a kind of effortless grace, a kind of wealth that I would have never been able to give her.

And yet again, I felt emasculated.

"First of all, Tony," Sienna said, reaching out to rest her hand next to my bowl of cheesy pasta. "I want you to know I've already forgiven you."

She finally pulled her hand back, but I couldn't stop

staring at her fingers. Her nails were a mess. I even saw dirt beneath them. What the hell?

"You and I..." She hesitated, then shook her head slightly. "We were each other's perfect match in our unique wounds. But as healed individuals, our parting would have been inevitable."

I wanted to say, Okay, eat my food, and get the hell back on the road. But another part of me—one I didn't fully understand—wanted to know more. About them. About their life together.

And Alexander—he was studying me. He had me figured out, I could tell. He had probably had me figured out from the start.

"But I lied and schemed, and it cost me everything," I admitted. And the second those words left me, something inside me shifted. I felt... lighter. Less burdened.

"Yes," Sienna said immediately. "And I still forgive you for all of it. I only hope—"

She frowned, hesitating. That hesitation was still so her.

Then, without my prompting, she added, "Heal, Tony. I hope you truly heal."

Then, we ate and talked, but frankly, I was distracted—disturbed, even. After lunch, they took me on a tour of their estate. We wove in and out of climate- and soil-controlled crops, moving through rows of greenery cultivated with precision. The more ground we covered, the more questions I asked, the more impressed I became by Alex's mission.

"If you own land, then do something with it," he said with a passion that caught me off guard.

I had always thought he was a bit of a poser, some billionaire playing philanthropist for good PR. But no—this guy was the real thing.

And Sienna… Sienna had changed too.

I learned her nails were soiled because she had been working in one of the glass containment houses before I arrived. And when she looked at Alex, her eyes didn't shine with blind admiration or worship. They shined with safety and partnership—with a deep, unshakable fondness.

She liked him.

He liked her.

That was real.

My crash into rock bottom didn't happen in their presence—it happened on the drive back to LA. The moment I pulled out of their gates, a dull ache settled in my chest. A longing. A loss.

By the time I hit the highway, my vision had blurred. My breathing turned shallow, ragged. I gripped the wheel tighter, trying to control whatever the hell was unraveling inside me.

I made it about twenty minutes before I had to pull over.

And then, I lost it.

I pounded my fists against the steering wheel—once, twice, three times—before slumping forward and hugging it, my body wracked with sobs.

That moment, broken and alone on the side of the road, was the beginning of my new future.

CHAPTER SIXTY-THREE

TONY

Today, the small bump in Sienna's stomach is visible when she meets me at the door in oversized jeans and a white tank top, smudged with dirt. She's been working on the crops again.

We hug, and as I pull back, I rub her belly with a grin. "Wow, you're nice and pregnant."

"It's a boy," she says, almost breathless with excitement. "We're calling him Gus."

I follow her out to the patio for lunch, and on the way, she tells me Alexander won't be home until tonight. That's fine. I have no agenda—my agenda days are long behind me, swallowed up by steady, twice-a-week therapy sessions with Ethan.

"How was your tour with Alex?" I ask, remembering that she's only been back in the States for a week. They spent three months traveling the world on a *Cooperative Climate Action Initiative* tour.

Sienna claps her hands in excitement. "Oh! I have to

show you something." She dashes inside and returns with a tablet.

Soon, we're watching footage from the documentary being put together to showcase the progress they've made. They sailed through tropical islands during what used to be hurricane season—only now, for the first time in decades, there's no devastation. No monstrous storms. Countries have finally decided to work together to save their world.

When the video ends, Sienna puts the tablet aside, and we dig into lunch—one of my favorites: orange chicken and vegetable stir-fry over perfectly cooked jasmine rice.

"So, what about you?" she finally asks between bites.

I smile as I load my fork again, because for once, I'm content with my answer. "I landed a big account."

Her eyes light up. "Oh, nice!"

I nod. "Yeah, I hired some help, too. I have a team now—four people."

"Small but steady wins the race," she says encouragingly.

"Indeed," I agree.

Then, she tilts her head, her voice turning softer. "But what about your love life, Tony?"

I press my lips together, exhaling slowly. I knew that's what she really meant. She wants to see me happy, to see me in love for real. I like that she wants that for me. She loves me, and I love her too—only this time, we love each other in the right way.

"I don't know, Sienna," I finally admit. "I have a

match string with YPM, but... my match hasn't used the service."

Her brows knit together. "But what if they never sign up? That happens, you know."

I take a moment to consider her question, gazing out over the estate—the perfectly cultivated fields, the house with its terracotta floors and wide windows that open to the outdoors. Happiness lives here. Love exists in every niche and cranny of this place.

Maybe that's why I love being here with them— Sienna and Alex.

They're living it—the kind of connection the creator of humanity intended.

Could I live the rest of my life without it?

My throat tightens, and I finally look back at her.

"I don't know, Sienna," I'm forced to admit. "I truly don't."